RU

Hot Ice #7
By Lily Harlem

Other Romance Books By Lily Harlem
Cold Nights, Hot Bodies
Breathe You In
Rule Breaker
HOT ICE series
THE CHALLENGE series
The Mobster's Girl
Scored
Thief
Her Dominant Billionaire
Stockholm Surrender
Chains of Command
Accelerated Passion

Chapter One

"Really? Are you sure?"

"Yes. They always come out of this door. Trust me."

I looked at Harmony, wondering if this was worth my while. We only had a twenty-hour layover in Orlando and hanging around the back door of an ice rink wasn't my idea of spending the time wisely. I'd much rather be perusing the malls and outlets for designer bargains. But she seemed obsessed with the Vipers, and one goaltender in particular.

"Jackson is just so sweet," she was saying, twisting her hands together beneath her chin, her long fuchsia-pink nails tapping together. "I know he's still a rookie, but wait 'til you meet him. He's destined for great things, really he is. You can see it in his eyes."

"Mmm, that's nice." Ice hockey wasn't my specialty. As a native English girl working for an American airline US sport did this to me on occasion—threw me into an alternative universe that I didn't quite understand.

"Nice," she said. "Seriously, Samantha, you need to clue up on this kind of stuff. He's so much more than *nice*."

The heavy red door pushed open and a couple of huge guys with sports bags slung over their shoulders wandered out. One had jet-black hair with dense stubble tracking down his jawline and over his throat. The other was blond, the thick strands were just starting to form cherub-like curls that somehow didn't match his enormous width and bulging biceps.

"Ladies," the blond said with a grin and a wink.

"Hi," Harmony simpered. "How's it going?"

"Be better when I've been fed," he replied with a laugh and continued to walk past us.

"That's all you think about, Brick," his teammate said in a gravelly voice. "Your damn stomach."

3

"No, there's another thing that plays on my mind regularly," Brick replied, slapping the taller man on his shoulder and laughing again. "I'm sure you can guess what."

"Yep, and no doubt she's waiting for you at *Ciao*."

They both chuckled in a sinful, rumbling kind of a way and headed into the lot.

I leaned back on the railings and watched them wander off—two seriously cute denim-clad butts that almost made it worth hanging around in the sun.

Almost.

"That was Brick," Harmony whispered. "He's so cute, and the other one, that's the captain, Ramrod. Phew, I wouldn't push him out of bed on a cold night." She giggled. "Or on a hot one come to think of it."

When her dirty laughter died down, I said, "They go for strange names, don't they?"

"They're not their real names," Harmony replied, tutting. "Just nicknames, you know."

"Mmm." I watched as Brick climbed onto a large orange motorbike, shoved on a black helmet and revved the engine. The sound reverberated around the hot asphalt and a haze of sizzling air shot from the exhaust.

Harmony returned her attention to the door that had closed itself on a heavy spring. She pushed her long, dark curls behind her ears and licked her glossy pink lips. She'd really had got herself in a flutter about meeting this hockey player. I wondered what she hoped would happen with him. He'd probably just nod hello like the previous players then be on his way and that would be that.

Whatever, I just hoped he wouldn't take too long about it. I was ready for a tall, cold drink. I shifted the strap of my purse on my sun-hot shoulder and crossed my ankles.

The door opened again.

Harmony perked up, puffing out her chest and cocking a hip.

A cleaner, carrying several swollen refuse bags, ambled past us. He was whistling a repetitive little tune and staring at his dirty sneakers.

"Duh, hurry up," Harmony muttered at the door.

"Shall we just go?" I asked. "They've probably gone home already."

"No, my inside source told me that they practice 'til three most days, it's only just past that now."

I held in a sigh and watched as the orange motorbike raced around a large black wagon then out of the lot. Either Brick was a speed junkie or he really was in a rush to get to whoever was waiting for him.

A slight rattle alerted me to the door being opened again.

As I turned, Harmony drew in a sharp little intake of breath.

Again two big guys walked out. One in gray sweats, the other in jeans. Both were carrying sports bags.

"G'day," said the player with dark curly hair and wearing the sweats.

"Hey, Jackson," Harmony said.

She pulled in a deep breath and her breasts barely stayed contained within the tight, red vest top she was wearing. We'd had to buy it on the way to the rink, especially for this moment, as it had a small Viper logo over the right nipple.

Jackson stopped in front of Harmony and pulled a pair of Ray-Bans from the v-neck of his t-shirt. He opened the slim arms and slid the shades on. Harmony's reflection filled the black lenses

"Ah, so you know my name," he said, "how about telling me yours, sugar? Even up the score."

She twitched her eyebrows and a rosy flush crept over her cheeks. "It's Harmony. Harmony Dale."

"Harmony." He grinned. "I'm sure you and I could make sweet, sweet music together."

She shifted from foot to foot and seemed to puff out her chest even more. "And we'd be perfectly in tune." She giggled and held up a pen. "Can I have your autograph, please? I'm a big Vipers fan."

"I can tell." He took the pen and used it to point at the logo on her top, hovering it just an inch away from her breasts. "And I'm always happy to oblige a big fan, especially such a pretty one."

I held in a sigh and fiddled with the St. Christopher pendant I wore around my neck. I glanced at the other player. He had a half-smile on his face and was playing with a set of keys, spinning them around his big fingers and catching them intermittently in his palm. His hair was super-short and white blond. His eyes, a soft blue velvet-color, sported light brown lashes and his mouth was wide, a bit too wide for his face, but it looked soft and sensual. His neck was thick and led to colossal shoulders and arms with such protruding muscles it appeared impossible for his upper limbs to lie flush with his body.

Damn, and what a body. A little frisson of interest fluttered in my stomach. It had been a few months since I'd enjoyed company in my bed—a one-night stand, who'd turned out to be a damp squib when it came down to business. He just hadn't kept up with me.

I licked my lips. I'd bet my best pair of Jimmy Choos that this guy would be the complete opposite to that non-starter and more than capable of matching my pace. I could almost smell the pheromones oozing from him and wow, those jeans sat nice on his hips—they hugged his groin in all the right places and held some interesting bulges and creases.

"Oh, damn, I don't seem to have any paper," Harmony was saying, tapping the pockets on her short white skirt in an exaggerated manner. "How silly of me."

"Then we'll have to improvise," Jackson said, sticking the pen in his mouth and pulling the lid off with his teeth.

"Oh, what do you suggest?" Harmony asked, batting her eyelashes.

He waggled the tip of the pen in the air and then angled it at her chest, speaking around the lid, "It may have to be a skin autograph."

"Well that's a good idea," Harmony said, stepping closer and tugging her top so that the swell of her breasts, and the top arc of her nipple, were completely visible.

I resisted shaking my head. She really was incorrigible. But who could blame her? With our brief few hours on the ground, if she didn't move quickly it wouldn't happen. Nothing would *ever* happen. The life of an international flight attendant was one that required snap decisions and lots of action. Sleep was usually the priority so free time wasn't something we had in abundance. Just as well I was due a weeks' leave in two days. Bliss. I couldn't wait. I'd head down to Miami for some fun, hit the malls and the pool big time.

As Jackson leaned in close and slowly scrawled his name on Harmony's flesh, I looked at the tall player in front of me again. He was still kind of smiling at me but now he also had a sinful glint in his eye, one I recognized. He liked what he saw. He liked me, or rather, my tight pink top, denim Donna Karan hotpants and waist-length hair. A swell of triumph grew within me, because that was just fine—I liked what I saw, too.

"There we go," Jackson said, replacing the lid on the pen. "How's that?"

Harmony glanced at her chest. Her brunette locks fell forward and tumbled over the signature. "Wonderful. Thank you."

Jackson shifted his bag over his shoulder and frowned. "What you gonna do when you shower?"

Harmony pouted. "I don't know. I'll be sad to see it go."

"Then you should come home with me so I can redo it, later that is, after you've showered." He held out his hand to her and raised his eyebrows.

"Well that *would* be a solution," she said, smiling coyly and delicately resting her hand in his.

He raised her knuckles to her mouth and kissed them. "I'd hate to leave a fan wanting," he murmured. "Or disappointed."

"Oh, I'm sure you'd never do that," she said.

"Not a chance."

Harmony giggled and turned to me. "I'll catch you later, Samantha. I'm going with Jackson, so he can redo this and—"

"Yeah, sure." I gave her a have-fun smile and waved her away.

She didn't need telling twice and turned, tottering off on her patent-red Vera Wangs.

Jackson slipped his arm around her waist and she bumped hips with him before gluing herself to his side.

She'd have a wild evening, no doubt, and who could blame her for grabbing the opportunity? She was young, free and single and knew what she wanted—a woman of the twenty-first century.

"Vadmir," the man in front of me said, holding out his hand. "My name is Vadmir Arefyev."

I tore my attention from the departing couple and let his warm fingers wrap around mine. He had a few callouses on his palm and his nails were neat and square-shaped. "Samantha." I paused. "But I guess you know that because my friend just said it."

"Yes." He grinned, a proper smile this time, not the half-amused curl of his lips he'd had before. "But you have lost your friend." He spoke with an accent, Russian I guessed, having heard passengers speak that way.

He released my hand.

"I've only lost her for a few hours." I knotted my fingers together, trapping the warmth infused from his palm. "Let's hope she doesn't eat him alive."

He laughed, a deep, rumbling chuckle that shifted his huge pecs beneath his t-shirt. "I hope she does. Jackson is still getting used to his new Viper fame and it might teach him a lesson. Knock him up a peg or two."

"Do you mean *down* a peg or two?"

"Yes, yes, that is what I mean, down." He smiled again and I noticed that his two front teeth were slightly crossed.

"Yes, he's new, isn't he?" Harmony had mentioned that earlier. "In that case, he might be a little worn-out at practice tomorrow."

He rubbed his hand over his chin, creating a sharp sound over his dusting of pale stubble. "I'm not here tomorrow but it would be good to see." He nodded at the parking lot. "So do you need a ride now?"

"I'll grab a cab, that's how we got here."

"I don't mind taking you somewhere. I've finished for the day."

"No really, I don't want to bother you."

"It is no...er...bother." He gestured to the lot. "Anyway, there are no cabs here."

"I'll call one."

"That will take a lot of time, and standing in this heat." He shook his head. "Not good."

As he'd spoken, a small, hot breeze lifted my hair from my shoulders and wafted the scent of dew-coated moss and light herbs my way. He was wearing an unusual cologne that seeped into my nose and heightened my awareness of his magnetism. There was definitely something seriously sexy about Vadmir Arefyev.

Damn, I really should get a ride out of here.

In fact, better still. I should make *him* my ride.

"Well I guess you're right," I said, "there are no cabs, so yes, a ride would be cool. As long as you don't mind."

"I really don't mind." He adjusted his bag, his upper arm muscles straining against the sleeve of his t-shirt. "It's this way."

He turned to the lot and I fell into step beside him. I had to take two strides to his one but luckily my Hermes wedges were up to the job.

He swung his keys around his fingers again. "Samantha, that is a pretty name."

"Thanks, yours is...unusual."

"Not where I'm from." He shrugged. "There are plenty of Vadmirs there."

"Where is that, then?"

He glanced at me. "You are not a Vipers fan?"

"No, sorry, I was just hanging out here with Harmony. I'm more of a Prada, Gucci and Jimmy Choo fan. Don't mind a bit of Donna Karan and Armani, either."

He chuckled again. "I get you."

"So you're from where exactly?" I asked.

"Russia. North of Moscow. I've been here four years now."

"Your English is good."

"Thank you. I have worked very hard to get it right."

"And do you miss home? Russia?"

He paused at a white convertible Chevy Camero and clicked his key fob. The car beeped to life and he tugged open the passenger door. "Yes, of course. I miss my family, my parents are not getting younger but at least, doing this, playing here, it means I can provide for them."

"That's very kind of you."

"They've always been very kind to me." He smiled and gestured for me to get into the car.

I climbed inside and he shut the door. As he walked around the front, I buckled up and placed my purse down at my side.

"And you," he said, dropping into the driver's seat. "You're not American. I can tell."

"Ah, well spotted. No, I'm English, well, technically half-and-half but I grew up in England so that's home. But my father lives over here, in Denver. America has been home, too for a long time now."

"We played Denver last month. I liked the cold. The heat in Florida can be very...tiring." He revved the engine and flicked on the air-conditioning.

"I won't disagree with you there." I crossed my legs.

His gaze drifted over my thighs and knees and I couldn't help yet another small thrill. It seemed Vadmir was a leg man, which was just as well. I had great legs. Not by chance but by hours in hotel gyms and a healthy dose of good genes from my grandmother and mother. Right now my legs were also tanned to a milky-coffee shade of brown.

"Tell me if you get cold," he said. "You're...er...not wearing much."

Now it was my turn to laugh. "I'm fine, it's a relief to be out of the sun."

He looked me in the eye and my breath hitched. There really was something captivating about him, and being this close to him—his handsome face, his scent and his obvious interest in me—was hitting all my buttons.

I pulled in a deep breath, licked my lips and willed my heart not to race too much.

"So where do you want me to take you?" he asked, his attention dropping to my mouth and his eyelids getting heavy.

On a fast and sweaty one-way trip to Heaven.

"I'm staying near the airport," I said, "so my hotel would be great."

He blinked, long and slow and I studied his lashes. "How 'bout we grab a drink on the way, Sammy?" He paused. "Can I call you Sammy?"

"Yeah, sure." I shrugged, feigning nonchalance because I was Samantha without exception—well, apart from now. And for some reason I didn't mind *Sammy* when he said it. Perhaps it was the accent. "And I guess we could grab a drink on the way, if that's what you fancy Vadmir."

Chapter Two

Vadmir took a right off the turnpike and pulled up to a small, wood-clad bar. It was fake Western complete with a rail to tie up non-existent horses, and had saloon-style doors. Above it a sign shaped like a spur read *Watering Hole*.

"Wait there," he said after he'd turned off the engine.

"Why?"

"Just wait." He unfolded his big body from the car and strolled 'round the front, his finger gliding over the bonnet. He then pulled open my door and held out his hand. "There you go."

I smiled. "I can open a car door, you know."

"I'm sure you can, but a lady shouldn't have to when there is a gentleman around."

Oh, he was a charmer all right. And with that spark in his beautiful blue eyes and that cheeky grin, he could be very dangerous indeed.

Or perhaps he could be just what I needed.

I took his hand. His hold was solid as I straightened.

"Phew, it's getting hotter out here," I said, "and it's only March."

"There's still thick snow on the ground in my hometown," he said, grabbing a dark green sports cap from the glove compartment. He pulled it low on his head and clicked his car locked.

"At least you get a few hours a day at the rink, in the cold."

"Yes, that time in the cold is good." He slipped an arm around my waist and urged me forward. He stooped slightly, as though trying to make himself inconspicuous, which was impossible given his size.

The Watering Hole was cool and dark and a familiar country song was playing on a jukebox. The floor was made of something designed to look wooden but felt like linoleum underfoot.

Vadmir dropped his arm from my waist as we walked toward the bar.

I missed his touch.

"What are you having?" he asked, looking down at me.

"A cola thanks."

"JD with that?" He tugged on his bottom lip with his teeth and appeared to be holding in a grin, as though daring me to throw caution to the wind.

"No." I smiled. "Too early in the day for me to hit the booze." Besides, if I was going to be lucky enough to get up close and personal with him, I wanted to be *compos mentis*, store the whole experience accurately in my memory to bring out on lonely nights and long flights.

"Two colas," he ordered, holding up his index and middle finger to the barman.

The barman stared at him for a second too long and then set to filling up a couple of tumblers from the draft. "Here," he said, sliding them toward us. "On the house."

"Nah, I'll pay," Vadmir said, shoving five his way.

The barman shrugged, took it and then pushed forward a pen and a cardboard bar mat. "Can I get your autograph? I root for the Vipers every game." He gestured to a board behind him. It was covered in red and white Vipers paraphernalia including a pic of Vadmir with his arm around the team captain who'd I'd seen earlier. They were both grinning broadly and their shiny black gum guards gave them a menacing appearance despite the obvious jubilation of the moment.

"Sure," Vadmir said, hovering the pen over the paper. "Who is it for?"

"Devon," the barman said. "Please."

Vadmir quickly scrawled on the mat and pushed it back.

"Thanks," the barman said, grinning and spinning to the wall behind him. He set about rearranging the existing pictures and newspaper clippings to accommodate the new autograph.

Vadmir picked up the colas and turned to me. "Quiet corner?"

"Yes, sounds good."

He led the way to what was indeed a dark and quiet corner. I took the opportunity to study his butt—it was high and taut and his jeans sat just right, and damn, he had long legs, like super-model-long legs, and I'd wager they were as solid as his arms were.

Feeling a little in awe of his physical size, I scooted into the booth opposite him and sipped my drink through the yellow-striped straw. He dropped his gaze down my throat and I wondered if he was watching me swallow—I wondered if he was imagining what it would be like to shove his cock in my mouth and come. Would I swallow then? Was his cock as big as the rest of him?

"So," I said, licking my lips. "What are the chances of your team picking up the cup this season?" Harmony had mentioned something about a cup, I was sure of it.

He cleared his throat and captured my gaze with his. "Good, more than good, things are going...swell."

"Swell, mmm...." Despite the cool drink I was hot and the word *swell*, damn, it made me think of swollen, engorged. Fuck, I was getting horny. I squirmed on the leather seat, plucked a band from my purse and set about scooping my hair onto the top of my head. I collected it in a thick ponytail then wound the band at the base.

Again he watched my movements, then took a long slug of his drink.

My breasts shifted beneath my t-shirt. He appeared to struggle momentarily on keeping his attention on my hair but then he gave in and his eyelids drooped and he watched my chest.

My nipples were tight and tingling and I knew without looking they'd be poking at my top.

"Phew, that's better," I said, "it's hot in here."

He grinned, slow and lazy, as if he had all the time in the world. "*You're* hot," he said, tipping his head and returning his attention to my face. "Like real hot, and real pretty, too."

"Why thank you." I steepled my hands beneath my chin and leaned forward on the table. I then studied the dampness on his soft bottom lip—a residual speck of moisture from his drink. "You're not so bad yourself."

He laughed, a low chuckle and winked. "So I've been told."

"I can't imagine a player for the Vipers doesn't know what he's worth. You must be very talented to be on the team."

"Yeah, I'm talented." He paused. "And not just at hockey."

I shrugged, trying to go for nonchalant, but I was enjoying our banter. "So what else can you do?" Jesus, I could just imagine.

He sat back and folded his arms, his knuckles pressing against his biceps. "Wanna find out...Sammy? Want me to show you what else I can do?"

My belly clenched and a quiver attacked my inner thighs. They were a loaded couple of questions that I didn't need decoding. He wanted to know if I was going to fuck him today. If I wanted to find out what else he was good at.

Hell yes.

I was a woman with needs and, from where I was sitting, I'd wager Vadmir Arefyev would be able to fulfill those needs and then some. Likely a few I hadn't even known needed attending to. I also had an empty evening ahead of me now Harmony had taken off, so what harm could a little company do? Hot, horny male company with no strings attached and a body of the incredibly lickable variety.

He was still studying me. His mouth had closed as though holding in more words as my brain formed an answer to his questions. Would I bolt? Slap him for his boldness? Or would I tell him that I'd been having dirty thoughts about sucking his cock for the last few minutes?

I reached for my drink again. Slurped up the last dregs of cola and then pushed it aside.

"My hotel is only five minutes from here," I said. "Is your place closer?"

He shook his head. "No, ma'am. It's about fifteen."

"Then we should go to mine and you can show me your other...skills." I paused. "I'm guessing you need privacy to do that."

"Privacy is a definite requirement." He unfolded his arms and leaned forward, coming so close to me I could smell his earthy cologne again. "I don't want Devon over there snapping pics of my naked ass for his memorabilia wall. My new boss, she would likely have something to say about that."

"I guess so." Now I knew, without a doubt we were on the same page. And thank the Lord for that, because I was going to get up close and personal with a sexy Russian ass and I could hardly wait.

* * * *

The drive to the Daylight Hotel took a grand total of four minutes. Vadmir was foot-to-the-floor the entire way. He didn't speak, just glanced at me a couple of times with a decidedly hungry look in his eyes.

But that was okay, because I was planning on letting him feast on me in the most unwholesome of ways. I just hoped he could walk the walk as well as talk the talk because I was buzzing for a bit of action.

He slammed to a stop underneath the hotel's covered entrance, tossed the keys to a valet and, after opening my car door, strutted through the automatic doors into the foyer with his hand pressed against the small of my back.

I glanced around, hoping to God I wouldn't see any of my flight team hanging about. I didn't. They were most likely at the malls or sleeping. Luckily I was an old hat at shift work and lived in my own time zone.

"The elevators are this way," I said, gesturing past a large urn holding orange and purple parrot flowers.

"Yup," he said in a grunting tone.

Vadmir stabbed the call button and the doors opened immediately.

We stepped in and the doors swished shut. As we were pulled up-ward silence surrounded us.

I looked at our reflections in the smoky-metal surface of the doors. I barely came up to his shoulder and was half his width, I'd guess I weighed a fraction of him and one of his legs was as thick as both of mine. A study of the bulge in his groin also told me that Vadmir Arefyev was primed and ready to go.

A small tremor of nerves fizzed through me and I clenched my fists. He really was enormous in every sense of the word.

He caught me staring.

"You still want to do this?" he asked, pushing his right hand into his jeans pocket and appearing to adjust himself.

"Do you?" I looked up into his clear eyes.

"I can't think of a better way to spend the rest of the day than with a hot chick." He paused. "And if naked is working for you, Sammy, then that's good for me." He turned from our reflections, rested his hand on my shoulder then smiled down at me, his whole face softening. "But if you want a movie and dinner that is cool, too."

His touch unleashed a craving deep inside of me, and I knew a movie and dinner wasn't going to cut it, not by a long shot. But it was sweet of him to suggest it.

I placed my hand over his, circled his wrist with my fingers then slid them up to his elbow, forcing the blond hairs back on themselves. His skin was soft but the tendons and roped muscles beneath were solid and thick. "Vadmir, I think we both know what we really want so let's not beat around the bush anymore."

"Beat around the bush?" He frowned a little. "What is that?"

"You know, pretend we want dinner and a movie when what we re-ally want is each other."

He grinned and the sinful glint returned to his eyes. "Ah, yes, okay. I understand what you are saying." He moved closer and slid his hand from my shoulder to the back of my neck. "No more beating the bush."

I was going to reply with a smart answer but I didn't. Instead I concentrated on him. Each one of his fingers pressed on my nape in a comforting yet possessive hold. He loomed over me, his scent and his body heat invading my senses. Up close I could see pale stubble covering the skin above his top lip and a tiny freckle to the right of his cupid's cusp.

I placed my hands on his chest. His pectoral muscles were wide and dense and pressed against the material of his t-shirt. I caught my breath and my breasts hitched.

He lowered his face to mine.

I leaned in, my concentration firmly on his mouth. Damn, I wanted that mouth on me. I wanted my mouth on him.

With a tinny ping the elevator doors slid open. He quickly released me and backed away.

I felt bereft. My heart was racing and my knees weak.

Quickly I gathered myself together. I had things to attend to and standing in an elevator wasn't going to get me anywhere.

"This way." I strutted out of the lift and along the carpeted corridor, being sure to wiggle my ass for his enjoyment.

He was close behind me, real close. I could hear him breathing. Luckily there was no one around because as we reached my door his hands were on my buttocks, groping and squeezing and exploring the shape of my hotpants and what was beneath.

My pussy clenched and heated. I fumbled with the keycard, but only for a moment because then I flung the door open and we tumbled inside.

A loud bang told me he'd back-kicked it shut and I found myself pinned against the wall by a very big, very hard hockey player.

I tilted my chin and stared into his eyes. "Bring it on," I said with a sassy grin as I pressed my breasts into his torso.

He hooked his arm beneath my right leg and pulled it up around his waist. His left hand was still on my ass.

"You sure?" he asked, his lips brushing mine and the stiffness of his cock pressing against my pussy through our clothes. "Are you sure you want to see what else I am good at?"

I tightened my leg around him and gripped his shoulders. "Hell yeah and get on with it. Show me what you Russian boys are made of."

Chapter Three

Vadmir's mouth hit down on mine. His tongue probed and explored and his rapid breaths blew hard on my cheek.

I gave as good as I got, slanting my head and greedily supping on his sweet yet masculine flavor. There was something exotic about him. He was mysterious and demanding and it was an intoxicating combination for a horny girl like me.

I wanted to touch him all over but didn't know where to start. He made the decision by dragging his top over his head. Our kiss broke and I feasted my eyes on his chest. Wide and defined, he had small pale nipples and a neat triangle of blond hair at his sternum. His skin was pale, despite him living in Florida, and I adored the creamy flesh that hugged his bricked abdomen. He had a thick patch of hair that led beneath the waistband of his jeans and there was a string of bruises around his lower right ribs, fading to blue and yellow and marking his otherwise unblemished skin.

"You like what you are seeing?" he asked, his voice hoarse and his lips rosy from the passion of our kiss.

"Are we playing show and tell?"

He curled his fingers beneath my top. "I guess we are." He pulled it upward and I raised my arms, glad that I'd matched my pale pink panties and bra that morning. They were Victoria's Secret and from this season's line.

"Mmm," he said, throwing my top to the side and dipping his finger into the lacy cup. "I like this bit you are showing."

"So look some more." I reached behind myself and unhooked my bra. It released and slid down my arms and I dropped it to the floor. My large breasts fell heavy and full and tingled with the cool air-conditioning washing over them.

His nostrils flared and he palmed the outer curves of my breasts. "*Yebat'*, you are beautiful."

20

I arched my spine and slid my hands up his neck and round to the back of his head. His hair was short and spiky and when he dipped to reach my breasts I pressed on his scalp, encouraging him to stoop farther.

He took my right nipple into his mouth and I gasped at the intensity. He'd created a sudden heated suction that sent shots of arousal through my chest and straight to my clit. I closed my eyes and groaned, held on to him all the tighter.

He laved and suckled, pulling my nipple almost to the point of pain, then switched his attention to the other breast and repeated the action.

My knees were like Jell-O. I'd lost contact with his cock. My vision wasn't focused but I spotted the bed. I needed him flat on his back. I needed to get better access and give him better access too.

"Over there," I gasped. "The bed."

In one swift movement he scooped me up. But I didn't have time to hang on because I was quickly deposited unceremoniously on top of the covers.

"Show me the rest," he said with a carnal grin.

"Only if you show me yours." I pushed a few loose strands of hair from my face and sat back on my heels.

He was already undoing his jeans, revealing black, tight boxers that left nothing to the imagination. As he shoved at the material he studied my breasts and licked his lips.

I licked mine as well. Damn, the guy was hung but I was no longer worried about his size. I was so turned on I knew I was going to have heaps of fun.

He kicked his boxers off then stood naked before me. His cock matched the rest of him—big and solid—and was rippled with delineated veins. His testicles, covered in the same pale hair as his abdomen, hung heavy beneath him and his thighs, two thick pillars of strength, pressed against the edge of the high bed.

I scooted forward and took hold of his cock.

He groaned and wrapped his enormous hand around mine.

I squeezed, just a little, familiarizing myself with his shape and density. "You have a big dick, Vadmir," I said, rubbing to the base then back up to the tip and relishing the marble-hardness.

"Yes, I have been told that before."

"I'm sure you have." I released him and moved backward on the bed.

He kind of growled as he followed me, his cock bobbing with his movements.

"Wait," I said, pressing on his shoulder. "Let me take these off."

"Quick or I'll rip them off."

"And then you'd have to buy me new ones." I reached for the button on my hotpants. "These are Donna Karan, you know."

"I don't care whose they are, get 'em off."

I kicked my wedged sandals to the floor, they landed with a couple of loud bangs, then I hastily shimmied out of my hotpants.

Vadmir was pushing at me, kissing my shoulder, tweaking my nipple, urging me flat on my back.

My breasts ached with need, my pussy was wet and my clit swollen against the material of my panties.

He curled his fingers into the waistband of my Victoria's Secret panties and tugged. A ripping sound told me the delicate lace hadn't coped with his energetic movements.

"Hey," I said, as he dragged them unceremoniously from my legs. "Watch it."

"I'll buy you more," he said breathlessly. "I'll buy you a hundred more pairs. A thousand if you want."

"Yes, you will—"

He cut my words off with a ravenous kiss as he pressed himself over me.

I squirmed against him, butting my chest into his and loving the sensation of flesh on flesh. The need to start my climb to orgasm was robbing me of breath and flooding my system with lust. Sod the panties, I could always buy more.

He slid his hand between my legs, ruffling through my thin landing-strip of pubic hair then edging into my folds.

I spread my legs and bucked my hips.

He found my entrance and pushed in.

I caught my breath and held it tight.

He groaned into my mouth and filled me again with what felt like two thick fingers.

I clenched around him. My moisture had eased his way and the rich scent of my arousal swirled between us.

"So hot," he murmured. "And fuck, you're going to be so tight wrapped around my dick."

"Yes, yes, give me more."

He withdrew a little then eased back in, fucking me with his hand. His palm caught on my clit and I ground against it, catching a spark of delicious pressure.

He kissed me again and I sank my nails into the flesh on his shoulders. The sheer size of him looming over me, blocking out the light in the room was a turn on in itself. I felt tiny beneath him, tiny and delicate but also hungry for the raw maleness of him that was such an opposite magnetism to my own.

"Ah, I'm going to make you come so hard and so many times," he said, against my cheek. "It will be so amazing for you. The best ever."

"Yes, yes, I..." My belly contracted and my thighs tensed. I knew it was coming soon. But it was *too* soon. I wanted to stretch out our fun.

I wriggled away from him.

He seemed surprised as his fingers slipped from my pussy.

I took advantage and pushed him to his back.

He fell willingly with a smile creeping over his face and balling his cheeks. "You wanna hop on for a ride?" he asked, holding his penis. "I promise it will be a good one."

Jesus, he was cocky and so damn sure of himself. I loved it. It was just what I needed. "Yes, but not your dick." I pushed to my hands and knees. "Grip the headboard, Russian boy."

He raised his eyebrows and also his hands then gripped the shiny wooden slats as instructed. He had a soft fuzz of pale underarm hair that I hurriedly settled my folded lower legs over, so I was kneeling with my spread pussy only inches from his face.

"Can you handle *this*?" I asked, looking down at his now flushed cheeks and his strong, straight nose.

He was staring at my intimate flesh. "I can handle anything you want to give me." He darted his tongue out and flicked it over my clit.

I gasped and grabbed the top rail of the headboard. It rattled against the wall.

"Mmm, you taste so sweet," he said, his hot breath breezing over my damp folds. "Give me more."

"Okay," I managed, lowering onto his face. I adored cunnilingus from this angle, it meant I had control over the amount of stimulation that on occasion was more than I could cope with.

Instantly he got busy with his tongue, rotating my clit with a perfect amount of speed and pressure.

I threw back my head and gyrated my hips. "That's it, just like that," I shouted sternly. "Don't stop. Fuck, don't stop."

My pussy was clenching around nothing, I bucked my hips forward and his tongue darted into my wet entrance; firm and long, he used it like a stubby cock to fuck me.

I murmured with pleasure and bobbed up and down on his face.

He raised his head, though he couldn't move his arms as I held him trapped, and again the bed whacked against the wall with a sharp bang.

My clit caught on the tip of his nose and, combined with his delving tongue, I found a blissful sensation. I kept on riding him, clinging to the shifting and rattling headboard.

"Yes, yes," I called, my fingers and toes curling as I climbed to orgasm. "That's it, fuck, I'm coming...I'm coming..."

I let out a long string of loud expletives as I came hard and fast on Vadmir's face. The moist sounds of his mouth and my pussy mixed as I pulsed through several violent contractions. I kept on grinding my clit on his nose, he didn't seem to mind, but then I did have him secured on the bed—though likely he could throw me off in a heartbeat if he wanted to.

Eventually the joyful sensations of my orgasm faded and I shuffled back, so that my wet, sensitive pussy was spread over his small patch of chest hair.

I placed my hands on the balls of his shoulders and looked down at his red, damp face. He too was breathing hard and his eyes were wild with desire, drinking me up. He released the headboard and rubbed his hands up and down my thighs and grinned.

There was a sudden furious loud thump on the wall, coming from the next room. "Oi, quit the fucking noise," a deep male voice shouted. "And the fucking banging."

I pressed my fingers to my lips and grimaced. Damn, we'd been a bit crazy then, or rather *I* had been. I'd gotten carried away with the moment.

Vadmir's expression lit in amusement. "That's what I like," he said, "*fucking noise* and *fucking banging.*"

"Yes, but—"

Suddenly he sat up and grabbed me around the waist. In an instant I was flat on my back staring up at him.

"Condom," I managed.

"Not time for that yet," he said, "I want my cock between your beautiful tits first."

"Yes, yes, do that." I was more than happy to get better acquainted with his cock.

"And I don't care how much noise and banging we make. You've got to live a lot, that's what I think."

"Live a little," I corrected.

"Nothing *little* happening here," he said, shifting up my body so that it was my turn to be pinned beneath him.

Fuck, he was right there. I eyed his cock, the slit was wide and deep and his glans was smooth as glass. He held it in his fist and lowered the tip toward my chest.

My mouth was watering to taste him so I reached forward, darted out my tongue and swiped it over the end of his cock.

He hissed in a breath through gritted teeth. "Go easy, Sammy, I might just go off and surprise you."

I smiled up at him and cupped his testicles in my hands. "Go ahead and surprise me then. Let me taste you properly."

He leaned forward, grasping the headboard that did its predictable shunt against the wall.

I opened my mouth and hoped he'd go easy on me. I didn't fancy choking on his big shaft.

He eased the head of his cock between my lips, just an inch, and then very gently, very slowly slid over my palate. His movements were the complete opposite to my frantic dance on his face. He didn't even hit my gag reflex, just filled my mouth for several blissful heartbeats and then withdrew.

"Hold your tits together," he said, sounding maddeningly in control.

I felt slightly aggrieved that I'd had such a small taste of his cock. I'd wanted more. But this was his turn to have the fun so I hoisted my breasts together and watched as he slid his now saliva-wet shaft between them.

He groaned long and guttural. A sound that didn't appear as controlled as he'd let on he was a moment ago.

"Ah, yeah," he said, slipping farther through the moist channel I was creating. "That's fucking amazing. *You're* amazing."

He pulled down and then slipped back up.

When the tip of his dick came within reach. I licked it.

He murmured something in Russian and set up a steady rhythm. I stared up at him. He was spectacular. Every muscle and tendon was hard and toned, his body better than anything I'd ever seen in a glossy magazine or on a catwalk.

"Vadmir," I said breathlessly, my fingers rubbing his cock as it slipped to the top of my cleavage. "I want you to come."

"*Dah, dah,*" he grunted then tipped his head back and blew out a long, labored breath.

I studied the angle of his chin, the groove beneath and the straining column of his throat.

A gloop of warm cum hit my chest, bursting from his cock in a long, pearly rope.

Again he shouted something in his native language, deep and raw and I could only guess that it was a particularly unholy praise to whatever god he believed in.

I clasped my breasts tighter around his cock and felt his shaft pulsate as yet more release shot from him.

He stared down at me, watching his semen splatter on my chest. His mouth was slack and his eyes wide.

"You look so hot like that," he said, panting as his movements finally slowed.

"Yes," I said, rubbing my index finger through the cum that sat in the well of my neck. "Covered in you."

I raised the warm drip to my mouth, sucked it in then hummed my approval at his taste.

He watched me, unblinking and then spread his mouth into another wide smile.

"Will you guys shut the fuck up or I'm calling reception," boomed the voice through the wall.

"Whoops." I giggled.

"Ignore him," Vadmir said. "He's just jealous."

Suddenly he reared back, scooped me into his arms and rolled over, so that I was pressed on top of him, my sticky chest rubbing up against his. "Because it's going to be a good night for us, and you, Sammy, can keep up with me just fine."

I kissed his mouth, over his cheek, then settled my lips at the shell of his ear. "I think what's more to the point, Russian boy, is are you are capable of keeping up with me?"

Chapter Four

The sound of the alarm tinkled into my dream about a party I was enjoying with friends from England.

I had no idea how long I'd ignored the buzzing, but when I finally came 'round, pressed against Vadmir's chest and with his seemingly constant hard-on nudging my thigh, I had an instant, heart-tripping panic about the time.

I rolled away from him and blinked open my eyes.

He murmured his displeasure and kept a tight hold of my waist.

I stretched and grappled for my phone.

"Shit," I shouted, unwrapping his arms and legs from mine. "Shit, I'm so fucking late."

"No, come back to bed." He didn't open his eyes but somehow managed to tackle me back beside his body. "Call in sick," he murmured, finding my mouth with his and palming my butt. "Let's stay here and keep doing what we're so damn good at. We're perfect together, Sammy."

I wriggled against him. "No, I can't ring in sick. I have to go."

He opened his eyes and stared at me. In the morning light the blue depths of his irises seemed even more intense than they had been when I'd first met him. "You sure?"

"Tempting," I said, interest tugging at my pussy. Damn, the man made me insatiable. "But I really I have to go." I had bills to pay, after all. An apartment deposit to fund.

He almost pouted but then sat sharply and released me. "What time is it?"

"Just gone seven."

"Fuck, I have to go." He leaped from the bed and began dragging his clothes on. "Fuck, fuck, fuck," he said, hopping around as he slotted his feet into his socks.

Naked, I darted past him and into the bathroom, flicked on the shower. As I stepped beneath the water the hotel room door slammed.

Good, he was gone. That meant I could get ready for work in peace. Pile up my hair and apply my make-up. Become Samantha the efficient flight attendant with a smile for everyone and not a curse word in my vocabulary or impure thought in my head.

So why did I feel deflated?

Because a goodbye would have been nice. After all, we'd banged until the headboard had lost a screw and the unhappy resident next door had either found some earplugs or moved rooms.

I lathered my body in Clinique shower gel and beat down my disappointment. Vadmir and *Sammy* had only ever been meant for a night of no-strings sex. I'd been lucky to find such a hot guy with awe-inspiring stamina. I should be thanking the heavens, not bemoaning the lack of a goodbye kiss. Because, after a string of disappointments, I was finally satisfied.

Thoroughly, utterly and thrillingly satisfied.

"Samantha, I thought you weren't going to make it," Harmony said as I dashed onto the 747. "You're never late."

"You know me, Miss Reliable," I said with a grin, scanning the empty fuselage. The cleaners were just leaving and everything looked in order.

"Did you see Patrick in the terminal?" she asked, straightening a few safety cards.

"No, I missed him."

"He was in high mood. I guess he got some, too, but I should warn you he's put you in the village today."

"Damn, really. I'm supposed to be in first."

"I don't know why you like first so much with all those stuck up passengers."

"You can't say that, and besides they're not as a rule. Just in a better mood because they're not packed in like sardines."

"I guess." She rubbed her hands together. "Week off soon, I can't wait to hit Miami."

"I know, me too." I sighed. "I hope there isn't a delay on the change over in New York like last week."

Our flight team did the international long-hauls and we'd be going all the way to Moscow in the next eighteen-hour shift. It didn't help that I was tired at the start. Tired but in a good way.

"He'll be here soon with the status," Harmony said.

"Who?"

She frowned. "Patrick, he's just sorting out some issue with the blue juice."

"Ah, okay." I paused as she turned to me.

Her make-up, like mine, was perfect. Her glossy red lips held the optimum shine and her kohl and mascara applied with precision. Her skin was flawless and complimented the dusky gray and brown shades of powder swept over her eyelids.

She saw me looking and swept her hands down her navy and scarlet skirt suit. "What?"

I grinned. "Did you have fun last night? With Jackson?"

She grinned, and beneath the foundation I spotted a subtle rise of color on her cheeks. "Damn yes, the guy is hung like a stallion and has the stamina of one, too." She giggled but then straightened her face. "Sorry to...you know, bail out on you like that at the rink."

I shrugged and plucked a speck of white fluff from her shoulder. "No worries, I had things to do."

"Mmm, I bet they weren't anywhere near as much fun as the things I had to do." She tugged her lip with her teeth and winked.

"No, I'm sure." I squeezed past her. "Tell me all about it later. I'd best get organized, the pax will be boarding soon."

The next hour sped by in a blur. I was responsible for more passengers in standard class and that required careful planning. Flying, I'd found, would often make people cranky so everything I could do to make their experience better was not only part of our airline's ethos but also part of my role.

Before long, the passengers began to board and Patrick and I stood at the tail end of the plane greeting everyone and doing a final boarding-pass check.

Patrick was tall and lean and spoke in a singsong voice. He was an amazing cabin steward, stayed calm in a crisis, could sweet talk the most irked of passengers and ran his team with consistent fairness. I liked him a lot and was happy to call him my boss.

Finally, all the passengers had stowed their baggage, strapped themselves in and were ready for the safety demonstration.

Patrick and I were looking after standard class, two more members of the flight crew were organizing business customers and, behind a thick curtain, Harmony and another colleague were responsible for first class.

After demonstrating how to don a life jacket, add more air, find a torch and blow a whistle, I stashed away my equipment. I had a quick check in the galley to ensure all was in order with the meals then took my seat for takeoff.

Patrick sat opposite me as we taxied along the runway.

"So did you go out last night?" he asked.

"No, I just stayed in my hotel room," I said, smiling sweetly. "Caught up on some personal stuff, went online, you know. I'm supposed to be looking for a new place to live. What about you?"

"Yeah, I went downtown, hooked up with an old friend."

"Friend with benefits?" I asked, with a conspirator-like waggle of my eyebrows.

He pursed his lips. "Well, wouldn't that be telling?"

I grinned. "Indeed." I'd bet though, like Harmony, although he thought he'd had fun it would have been nothing on mine. I'd had an amazing night with Vadmir. One of the best ever. He'd had so much energy, every time I'd thought we'd finished fucking he'd got it up again. We'd done it missionary, doggie-style, and I'd ridden his cock 'til I couldn't catch my breath then he'd had me up against the wall, hanging onto the headboard. That was when it had lost a screw.

"Did you get the blue juice sorted?" I asked as the pilot romped up the speed and I was pressed back in my seat.

"Yes, it's that one loo at the back. Always seems to need more fluid than the rest."

"Yes, I've noticed that." I glanced over his shoulder at the rows of heads wobbling as the plane hurtled to full ground speed. I didn't even notice takeoffs and landings anymore; I'd done so many of them. We were trained for any eventuality but the truth was we hardly had to use the majority of our skills, which was just as well because they were for emergencies, life or death situations.

Within a few minutes the captain came on the tannoy announcing that cabin crew could release. Patrick and I unclipped, folded our seats away and began organizing the drinks trolleys.

As I bent and stretched I was aware of a few muscle aches here and there. My hips had had a good workout being wrapped around Vadmir, and my shoulders hurt from gripping the headboard. At one point I found myself staring out of the galley window at the coastline below, thinking about how I'd sat on his face, how the tip of his nose had been the ideal buffer for my clit as he'd poked his tongue into my pussy.

A little shiver attacked my spine and my internal muscles clenched. Damn, that had been hot. He'd been all for it, letting me pin him down like that and take what I wanted.

"Hey, Samantha, are you okay?"

I turned to Patrick who was decanting ice. "Yes, fine, why?"

"You're lost in your own little world."

"Just a bit tired, I guess."

"Hmm," he said, giving me a suspicious look.

"What?"

"I thought you had an early night?"

"I did."

He turned back to the ice. "You can take first break if you want."

Kennedy was only four hours away but once the passengers were fed and settled into a movie we usually took it in turns to have a fifteen minute break, unless it was super-busy.

"Yes, I might just take you up on that offer," I said. Although I'd been in bed early, I hadn't had much sleep and that was definitely starting to take its toll.

By the time we reached New York and disembarked the passengers, Harmony was feverish and waves of nausea were washing over her. We'd been so busy I hadn't had chance to take a break or catch up with her during the flight as I usually did so I was shocked by her sudden, sickly appearance.

"You should stay on the ground," Patrick said to Harmony as she sat fanning herself with an inflight magazine.

"I'll be fine," she replied, closing her eyes and leaning back in the first-class seat. "Besides, we've still got the longest leg of the flight to do, you can't be one down in first."

"I'm sure we can figure something out," Patrick said, frowning.

"No, I'm fine, really." She shivered. A sheen of perspiration had formed on her brow, melting her make-up.

"What has made you so ill?" I asked, glad that the passengers wouldn't witness her vomit. She looked about to hurl and she was a nasty chalky color.

"I don't know. Jackson and I ordered take out last night, we...you know, built up an appetite. I think maybe the shrimp wasn't as fresh as it could have been."

I grimaced. "In that case, you really shouldn't be embarking on twelve hours in the air."

"I agree." Patrick put his hands on his hips and tilted his chin. "Executive decision. Harmony, lay over in one of the hotels, you're in no state to be serving food."

"But—" she said, frowning and then swallowing as though she had a nasty taste in her mouth.

"No buts," Patrick said. "You're off this flight crew. I'll call Nina at HQ and tell her we're short on the next leg because of illness. See if she can rustle someone up for us."

"Samantha could switch to first," Harmony said, looking at me with wide eyes.

Patrick sighed. "Yes, would you, Samantha? It'll make us a bit short at our end but we'll manage if HQ don't deliver us someone."

"I don't see why not." I held in a grin of delight. First was much sweeter and where I felt at home, or at least at work.

"Thanks, guys," Harmony said, "But I really hate leaving a crew short, I know how much extra work it is when we're one down."

"We'll manage," I said, "And you need to be lying in the cool somewhere. Maybe just sip water for the next twelve hours."

"Yes, I think I will," Harmony said then clasped her hand over her stomach. "Oh God, the cramps have started."

"Go. Now," Patrick said.

Harmony nodded. "Yes, yes, I will." She stood and gripped the corner of the wall.

I handed her flight bag over. "Do you want me to help you?" I asked.

"No, I'll be fine, but..." She paused and pressed her fingers over her lips.

"Would you just get out of here," Patrick said, pushing her toward the exit. "I don't want to clean up your mess. And stay away from shrimps in the future."

Harmony took a deep breath, appeared to compose herself, and then headed down the steps onto the tarmac.

"Christ on a motorbike," Patrick said, "I thought she was going to cover us then."

"I hope she makes it to the hotel," I said, watching her go and toying with my St. Christopher.

"The ground crew will see that she does, I'll radio ahead and warn them. She can sleep it off and we'll pick her up when she's better." He rubbed his hands together. "Right, we'd best get to it, they'll be boarding again soon and we need to get across to gate six."

After grabbing my overnight bag, I made my way to gate six with the rest of the crew and boarded the plane that would be taking us across the Atlantic to Moscow. As I moved to the front of the fuselage I felt happier with each step. This would be a much sweeter trip in first class.

I'd just freshened up my make-up when the co-pilot stepped out of the cabin. He wasn't particularly familiar to me, he was one of those who stood in for holidays and sickness, and I'd only met him a couple of times.

"Hello," he said and glanced at my badge. "Samantha."

"First Officer Jones," I replied, "Can I get you something?"

"Yeah, do you have some aspirin? I've got a pounding headache."

"Yes, of course. Anything else?"

"Some water, too, please." He rubbed his temples.

"Is it serious?" I asked, hoping that we weren't about to lose another member of the team.

"No, I'm just tired. Didn't get much sleep last night."

"Oh, really." I smiled as I reached for a bottle of still water. "Out partying," I joked.

He huffed. "No, I was on a layover in Orlando but the couple in the room next to me were at it 'til about four in the morning. The Daylight Hotel has such damn thin walls."

My heart tripped. That was about the time Vadmir and I had finally collapsed in our room. The same damn hotel. "I'm sorry to hear that," I managed.

He tutted. "Some folk just can't control themselves," he said, "They were banging against the wall, shouting very primitive demands and wailing, actually wailing, or at least she was. It sounded like a fabulous time for those involved, which I wasn't, so for me it was pretty damn miserable."

Oh fuck. Heat was rising on my chest, spreading up my neck and onto my cheeks. Quickly I reached for the medical kit and rooted around for painkillers. That damn headboard and its rattling. And why had I never been able to fuck quietly? I was a talker and a wailer and Vadmir had been only too happy to join in.

"Eventually," First Officer Jones said, "after they took no notice of me asking them to shut up, I resorted to earplugs. It didn't block it all out but reception said the hotel was full and I needed to do something."

"Yes, absolutely, and good idea." I stood, handed him the aspirin and gave him my best concerned expression. "I hope your headache goes away soon. It's beef in ale for main course today, is that okay?"

He sighed and knocked back the pills. "Yep, perfect. Let's just get this show on the road and be on our way to Moscow. I hope the hotel there will be quieter."

Chapter Five

I carefully popped the cork on a fresh bottle of champagne for the first-class passengers and then secured it in ice. My new co-worker, an older member of staff called Tara, had re-welcomed everyone on board and seen to the safety briefing for the new travelers who'd joined us.

I'd been busy in the first-class galley preparing hors d'oeuvres and silently panicking about First Officer Jones and his sleepless night—of all the luck to have him in the room next to me in Orlando. Usually we picked up new cockpit staff at Kennedy, but it seemed that wasn't the case today.

Damn it. Of all the bad luck.

What if he found out it had been me doing all that wailing and banging? I should have considered that it might be a member of airline staff next door. HQ blocked out sections of rooms for staff who were on layovers, on-call or just passing through. It worked out cheaper that way for all involved.

"Cabin crew for takeoff," First Officer Jones announced over the loud speaker. I glanced at the cockpit door. With a bit of luck he'd stay in there until his anti-fatigue rest.

Tara appeared in the galley and pulled the privacy curtain flush. Our first-class staff area was adjacent to the galley and out of view of the passengers.

"Is everyone settled?" I asked.

She tapped her hair, making sure no strands had escaped the French pleat. "Yes, fine. Nothing untoward, no crumb crunchers or special diets."

"That's a nice change." It was always a more settled fist class cabin without kids or faddy eaters.

We sat on our flip-down seats for takeoff. The engines revved and we began to hurtle along the runway.

"So what happened to Harmony?" Tara asked, glancing out of the small window.

"Bad shrimp," I said, pulling a face.

"Yuk."

"Indeed," I replied.

"So Patrick sent you to step into her shoes."

I grinned. "Well she did buy a very nice pair of Vera Wangs last month that I've got my eye on."

Tara laughed as we took to the air.

Within minutes we were leveling out and First Officer Jones switched off the crews' seatbelt sign and I unbuckled.

"Action time," Tara said, standing.

I did the same and reached for the drinks tray. I carefully secured three champagne cocktails within the spread of my fingers and headed out of the galley and into first class.

Here the chairs were large and deep and well spaced out so the passengers could stretch in their own private space complete with screen and power sockets. Right now it was midday and they were all plugged in or flicking through magazines.

"Champagne, madam?" I asked, holding the tray before a well-made up business woman.

"Thank you," she said, taking one. Her fingernails were a beautiful pearlescent pink and she wore a large ruby on her ring finger.

"I'll return with pre-dinner snacks in a moment," I said, "but don't hesitate to call if you need anything in the meantime."

She smiled and I moved to the customer at the window seat. He took a drink but barely lifted his face from his book. Nervous flyer, I suspected. Speed reading to keep his mind off the ascending plane.

The engines were still working hard, the floor on which I stood sloped heavenwards.

I moved to my next passenger with a bright smile on my face and words of welcome on my tongue.

My heart rate stuttered. I caught my breath. I reached out and gripped the headrest of the nearest chair.

Staring straight at me, from beneath a green cap, was my sexy hockey-playing Russian boy, Vadmir Arefyev.

His blue-velvet eyes were wide and his mouth slack. He was as surprised to see me as I was to see him.

And Jesus was I surprised. What the fuck was he doing here? Wasn't he supposed to be skating around a rink or something? Hitting pucks into a net?

"Champagne?" I asked, holding out the tray, my thumb still over the base of the glass to keep it secure. My whole arm was shaking and my throat was tight.

He took it without saying a word. The stem looked ridiculously delicate in his grip.

God, was it really him? Perhaps it was a lookalike?

"Sammy?" he said, twisting his mouth into that amused half-smile he was so damn good at.

Oh, it's him all right.

"We have beef in ale for main today or salmon with hollandaise," I said, swallowing. My mouth was dry and my knees a little wobbly. "And a selection of desserts to choose from. It's all on your inflight menu."

"What are you doing here?" he asked quietly and leaning his bulk forward in the seat.

"And if you need any assistance with working the personal screen, just let a member of crew know," I said, taking a step backward, toward the galley. "We're all happy to help."

Fuck. As if it wasn't bad enough that the First Officer had heard me wailing with ecstasy all night long, the man I'd been riding hard was here, sitting on our plane and would be for the next eleven and a half hours.

This couldn't be happening. Vadmir and I were supposed to be a one-night stand—never to see each other again and left only with toe-curlingly, sumptuous erotic memories.

He frowned and with his free hand gripped the arm of his seat, his huge fingers curling around the end.

Heat rushed up my chest and neck and onto my cheeks as I recalled him ripping my panties off and sliding those fingers into my slickness. Damn, he'd known just how to make my body sing.

Quickly I retreated into the safety of the galley and pulled the heavy curtain across the archway. I needed a moment to gather myself before I served the other passengers. Tara was hosting the right-hand side but this section, but here, on the left, these travellers were mine. *He* was mine. My responsibility.

Why the hell didn't Harmony warn me?

I set the tray down and buried my face in my hands. Harmony hadn't even known I'd spent the night with Vadmir. We'd barely said a few words to each other all day and then she'd become sick. How could she have known to warn me?

The curtain swished back and I startled, pressing my hands to my chest.

"You okay, Samantha?" Tara asked, coming to an abrupt halt. "You look like you've seen a ghost."

"No, I'm fine, really."

If only.

She frowned. "Don't tell me you ate the same shrimps Harmony did."

I shook my head. "No, not at all. No shrimps for me. I'm okay, honestly."

Quickly I re-loaded my tray. I'd just have to wear my most professional mask and get through this damn flight. Shit. If only I'd stayed in standard class with Patrick. I wouldn't have ever known Vadmir was on board. Not only that, I wouldn't have had to see First Officer Jones and find out about his sleepless night.

What a mess. Could I feel any more embarrassed?

Tara had gone again, serving her passengers drinks and snacks with her usual efficiency.

I took a deep breath and stared at the curtain. Much as I wanted to I couldn't hide in the galley for an entire flight. And why should I? We'd both known what we were doing. No strings sex, that was all. Really fucking good sex but still, no ties afterwards. We were both adults, right? We could move on from this with no ill effects.

With my chin tilted I moved down the aisle again. I tended the man opposite Vadmir with a smile and a polite remark. He took his drink and I promised to return with water so he could take a pill.

As I spoke I could feel Vadmir's gaze on me. If he reached out, across the aisle, he'd be able to stroke my ass, the way he had in the corridor the night before as we'd tumbled into my room. But now I didn't wear hotpants—now I had on a navy, pencil-straight skirt that fitted me like a second skin and a tight-fitted jacket that nipped in at my waist and skimmed neatly over my breasts.

Now I was in work mode, a professional and he'd have to accept that.

I worked my way farther along the aisle, tending everyone, and then slipped back toward the galley. When I walked past Vadmir, so close I could smell that damn gorgeous cologne he wore, again I knew he was staring at me—at my ass as my hips swayed with each step.

Was he remembering how he'd bent me over the bed and fucked me as he'd gripped my hips to keep me just where he'd wanted me? Damn, I reckon I had two sets of bruises from his fingertips. We'd gotten pretty carried away on that particular occasion.

Hurriedly I pulled the curtain across, glad to be out from under his scrutiny. A mass of memories were billowing in and out of my mind like a jumbled blur from a porno movie. I was hot and flustered.

Tara was heading out with a tray of pre-dinner snacks. I was behind with my serving but that didn't matter.

I moved to the window and flapped the top section of my blouse, breezing it beneath my jacket. Why was it so warm in here?

I stared downward. Beneath me cotton wool clouds ballooned together, an undulating surface for us to skim over. Below the clouds the Atlantic was stretching out before us, a vast expanse of water waiting for us to cross.

The hostess buzzer pinged and I glanced at the screen. It was my passenger who wanted the water. Patience clearly wasn't his strong point.

After reaching for a bottle of Evian and a tray of snacks I moved back into first class. I delivered the water and then set about handing out hors d'oeuvres. The business lady took two and the nervous flyer waved his hand at me, refusing even a nibble.

Bracing myself and plastering on my most professional smile, I turned to Vadmir.

Damn, the guy was sexy. He'd done a casual destruction of his clothing since I'd last looked at him. His cap was twisted to the side, the top button on his black Polo shirt was undone—the collar a little curled—and he'd un-tucked the base of it from his jeans. I itched to straighten the collar but resisted. Last night I'd had permission to run my hands, and my tongue, all over him. But that was last night and this was now. Now he wasn't mine to touch.

"Would you like something from the tray, sir?" I asked, lowering it in front of him.

He didn't even glance at the carefully prepared canapés, instead he stared, unblinking, straight into my eyes.

"Sir?" I asked as my heart thrummed and that scorching flush of heat moved back over my chest. I tried to beat it down but he was soul-achingly handsome and I was finding it hard to speak, hell, breathing was difficult. "Can I tempt you with something?" I managed.

"You know my name," he said in a low, rumbling voice as he narrowed his eyes. "Quit the sir thing."

"The thing is, *sir*," I said, "Right now I'm handing out food to passengers and you're a passenger."

"I am more than a passenger." His nostrils flared. "And you know it."

I gulped. He hadn't shaved—no doubt been in too much of a rush after our late start to the day—and he had a dusting of blond stubble over his jaw and chin, it was denser over his upper lip. It gave him a rugged, menacing look that combined with his accent and the steely glint in his eyes just made him all the more alluring.

"I take it you don't want anything," I said, refusing to think of him as alluring for another second. I was on duty and it just wasn't professional. "But if you change your mind please call for a stewardess." With my free hand I indicated the small red button set in the control panel on the arm of his seat.

Suddenly he dashed out his hand and wrapped his fingers around my wrist. He pulled me in close, so close so that I was leaning right in toward him.

I gasped and gripped the tray tight to prevent the contents from spilling. "What are you doing?" I whispered harshly as my nose almost touched his.

"You know my damn name, Sammy," he whispered, his hot breath spreading over my neck. "You were screaming it last night. Screaming it as I made you come so hard you could hardly remember what planet you were on..." He paused. "So use it. Say my name."

My stomach clenched.

He mashed his lips into a tight line, then, "Please," he said, softer this time, "don't make me feel like I was nothing more than a jock with a cock to you. That would be hurting my feelings very much." He frowned and swallowed.

A full body tremble attacked me. I gulped in a breath. "V...Vadmir," I said, nodding at his hold on me. "Let go of me...now."

He flashed open his fingers and released my wrist.

"Thank you," he said. "That was all I wanted."

Hurriedly I straightened, glanced left and right, and hoped no one else had seen our interaction. My heart rate settled a modicum. I'd gotten away with it. Everyone was tucked into their own little worlds.

"Dinner will be served soon," I said shakily and gripping the tray with both hands.

His gaze slipped downward to my breasts.

I stepped away and continued serving. I was glad it was nothing more complex than holding out fancy food. My nipples were tight, my body buzzing. My brain was on overdrive. Flashes of all the sweaty and naked things we'd done were holding my mind's eye hostage once again.

Damn it. I hadn't expected to see him for the rest of my life yet here he was, looking at me like he wanted a repeat performance and touching me in that sinfully commanding way of his.

I'd have to take a stern hold of myself and get through this flight. There was nothing else for it but to grit my teeth and cope.

For the next few hours I was glad to be busy, even though I could feel Vadmir's gaze on me every time I walked past, at least I had things to occupy my mind. Tara was easy to work with and with well-oiled efficiency we soon had everyone fed and settling down with blankets, movies and after dinner drinks.

"Do you mind if I take first break?" she asked as the sky outside darkened.

"Not at all...oh, have you collected all three trays from the cockpit?" I asked. Tara had conveniently fed the pilots, which saved me facing the First Officer again.

"Yes, all done, but Jones has a headache. He's going to the crew quarters for a lie down."

Another pang of guilt attacked me. "Oh, okay, I gave him aspirin earlier. It didn't help then."

"No, but a rest will do him good. And me, I'm exhausted." She reached for her small, airline issued purse. "See you in an hour."

"Yes, get your feet up."

Tara disappeared through the curtain, heading for a discreet, small door between first and standard that led to a cramped but adequate space for lying down and grabbing some sleep.

I turned to the window. The clouds had dispersed and the outline of Greenland was visible with startling clarity even though twilight was spreading fingers of orange red, and yellow over the horizon. Dragging in another deep breath, I stared at the ice crystals forming on the outside of the window.

There was a noise behind me—the swish of the curtain and footsteps.

I froze.

I could smell him again. His aftershave.

I spun around.

Vadmir was standing in the galley. His enormous shoulders almost spanning the gap between the stainless steel walls.

"You're not allowed back here," I said, folding my arms and frowning. "The cockpit is just there and this is for staff only."

"I wanted to see you." He tipped his head and raised his eyebrows. "Alone."

He took a step toward me, hemming me into the tiny space at the end of the galley.

I took a step backward and felt the rim of the window press against my shoulders. "You can't...it's against the rules."

He came closer still, pressed his palm against the fuselage wall by my right ear and leaned down until our faces were close. "The thing is, Sammy, I'm famous for many things and one of them is breaking rules."

He gave a sinful grin. "But I thought you would have guessed that by now."

Chapter Six

"Vadmir," I said, gulping in a breath. He used up all the space in the confined area, and it seemed all of the oxygen, too. "Please, I'm at work."

The evening light, seeping through the window, cast his face in shadow and beneath the rim of his hat his eyes had darkened to the color of the deepest part of the ocean.

"Yeah," he said, "I can see that and I like it." He reached out and touched the outer side of his index finger to my cheek, stroked from my ear to my chin and back again. "I like it a lot."

His gentle caress sent a whole load of white-hot sensations bursting through my system. I gripped the preparation surface to my right for stability. My knees were shaky.

"Sweet little sexy uniform," he murmured, darting out his tongue and licking his lips. "It's got me having all kinds of dirty thoughts about you while I've been sitting there, watching you, wondering...remembering."

"You shouldn't be thinking that way," I said as an insistent ache settled in my pelvis. He'd been having dirty thoughts about me. Remembering our time together. Well, yes, this was a sex-god hockey player I was dealing with, he was hardly reciting poetry in his head. "And you shouldn't be watching me, either," I managed.

"What else is there for me to do?" he whispered, "But think about what's beneath that damn tight skirt of yours and how willing you were to share it with me last night. Damn, we had fun, didn't we."

My heart stuttered. I couldn't deny the fun part, but then he hadn't said it as a question. He knew full well I'd had fun. "There's plenty to do onboard...watch a movie, read, listen to music. I don't know, think of something." I glanced around him at the cockpit door. It was thankfully still shut. "What happened last night between us is over. It was just sex, nothing more. I thought you understood that."

He moved his hand from my face to my waist and tugged me close, until my breasts pushed up against his chest and my legs touched his.

I clenched my fist against his shoulder in an attempt to keep him at a semi-safe distance but it was no good, his grip was firm, and beneath the material of his top he was as solid as I remembered. His possessive hold was also as pussy-dampening as my memories served me.

"Just sex," he whispered hotly against my cheek. "Yeah, it was just sex, but fuck me it was intense. You can't deny that, Sammy." He slipped his hand to the top curve of my butt and squeezed me closer still. "Intense for me *and* you."

A long hard wedge of flesh that I'd become acquainted with the night before lodged against my stomach.

"I'm not denying it," I gasped. "It was intense, yes, but it was just one night."

He touched his lips to my ear. His breaths were loud and warm and trickled over my scalp and down my neck. "One perfect night of ecstasy."

I shut my eyes and recalled the sound of him coming, of us coming together. For a moment I was back there, in the hotel room. We were hot, naked and writhing on the bed, as he'd just said, in ecstasy. I could still feel his thickly muscled arms and legs wrapped around me as his athletically-honed body drove us both to exquisite release. Fuck, his arms were around me now.

"Russian boy," I whispered, releasing my grip on the counter and clinging to his biceps.

"Sammy..."

I tipped back my head and breathed in his scent. I brushed my lips against his jawline, the stubble there was abrasive and sensual, and I allowed my weight to press against him.

He was right. It had been perfect. We'd been so in tune, so well matched in the bedroom. Almost like we'd rehearsed everything even though we'd never met before.

He let out a small moan as his cock ground against me through our clothes.

Lust was pouring through my veins now. I could make out the girth and density of him. My chest was tight and my pussy trembling. I was sure there'd be a small damp patch on my knickers. Damn, as if I hadn't got enough last night and here I was hungry for more.

A sudden sharp click rattled around the galley.

The cockpit door.

I opened my eyes and shoved at him. "Move!"

He'd already released me and taken a step back. With his arms at his sides and his cap pulled low he kept his gaze firmly on my face, apparently unconcerned by the telltale bulge in his jeans.

First Officer Jones stepped out, pressing his hat on.

"Oh, hello," he said, stopping and staring up at Vadmir who was easily a head taller than him. "I'd seen on the passenger manifold that we had an all-star on board. It's great to meet you." He held out his hand. "Blake Jones."

"Nice to meet you, sir," Vadmir said, shaking hands. "But who is flying the plane if you are standing here?"

First Officer Jones laughed. "Oh, don't worry, I'm one of the co-pilots, there are still two guys up front keeping an eye on things."

"Glad to hear it." Vadmir moved from one foot to the other.

Perhaps he was uncomfortable, after all.

"Could I could get your autograph? If you don't mind that is. My kid is a mad Vipers fan."

"Sure, what's his name?"

"Tristan." First Officer Jones turned to me. "Samantha, do you have a pen and paper Mr. Arefyev could use?"

"Certainly. I'll take it to his seat right now," I said, nodding at the curtain and indicating that Vadmir should return to his chair. That was a close enough call, he needed to get out of the galley.

"That's okay," Vadmir said, "I'll happily sign it here. I'm enjoying stretching my legs."

"Yes, it gets like that for big guys, even in first," First Officer Jones said. "But are you enjoying your flight so far? Do you have everything you need?"

"Oh, yes. I have everything I need." He settled his attention on me again. "I have everything I need right here."

"I'm pleased to hear it and it's awesome to meet you." He moved past Vadmir. It seemed the no-passengers-in-the-galley rule didn't apply to hockey players.

"Oh," First Officer Jones said, turning with his hand on the curtain. "One quick question."

My stomach swirled. Fuck, did he somehow suspect the two people standing before him had caused his sleepless night? And if so would he still be as charming and polite? Would he still want Vadmir Arefyev's autograph?

"Fire away," Vadmir said, continuing to study me with an expression that made me wonder if he was considering eating me the second the first officer went from the galley.

I leaned against the wall again and gripped the side of the counter, kept my attention on him.

"Who do you think...?" Jones looked between the two of us, his mouth set in a serious line.

I held my breath. Shit.

"Will lift the cup at the end of the season?" he said with a smile.

"Vipers of course," Vadmir said with a huff as if it were a stupid question. "No doubt about it."

"Yep, I agree," First Officer Jones said. "Let's hope you're not away from the team for too long, though. They've got a game tonight, haven't they?"

"They'll handle the Penguins without me just fine."

"Hope so." First Officer Jones slipped from the galley and with him went my invisible safety shield.

Damn, I'd nearly kissed Vadmir, a passenger, only moments earlier. That was a disciplinary offence, I was sure, or at the very least a caution. And it was very nearly an officer who'd caught us.

"You have to go," I said in a harsh whisper.

He raised his eyebrows.

"Now, please. Return to your chair."

"I will if you tell me one thing?"

"No, under aviation law, if a member of crew tells you to do something, you must do it. Go sit down."

He grinned in a maddening way. "Oh, I love it when you get all bossy with me, just like you did last night when you flipped me on my back, shoved my hands over my head and rode on my face, that was just so—"

I marched up to him and slapped my hand over his mouth. "Shut the fuck up."

Amusement sparkled in his eyes and beneath my palm I felt his mouth stretch into a grin.

Damn, I wanted to tie him up and tease him 'til tomorrow and back for that remark. Make him pay for saying those words out loud, up here, on my flight. "Shut up and sit down. I won't tell you again." Carefully I lifted my hand from his mouth. Moisture from his lips made my skin tingle.

"Yes, ma'am," he said. "If you can do one thing for me."

"What?"

"Give me a quick kiss. I missed out on a goodbye one, we were both in such a rush to catch this flight."

"No, out of the question, not at all. I—"

My words were cut short as he swept me up against him and pressed a wild, ravenous kiss to my lips.

I wanted to squeal in protest but couldn't risk anyone discovering us. And damn, the guy could kiss. His soft lips were pliant yet firm. He tasted divine, champagne and man, an intoxicating combination.

But still I didn't give in completely and I writhed against him as he pulled me onto my tiptoes, deepening the kiss and slanting his head as his tongue tangled with mine.

I gathered his top in my fists, both wanting to pull him closer and shove him away. My mind was spinning. What was it about him that made me throw caution to the wind?

As suddenly as he'd snatched me to him he released me. I stumbled backward and clutched the counter. My lips felt bruised, my heart was racing and heat was burning between my legs.

He had smudges of lipstick over his mouth, bright sticky red lipstick that looked all the more startling on his pale skin.

"Just so you know," he said. "That wasn't a goodbye kiss."

"What do you mean?" I managed, pulling in breaths that made my erect nipples scratch against the inside of my bra.

"That was just to remind you what you could have again...later."

"Later!" I shook my head. "Are you always this cocky?"

He reached forward, his eyes blazing. "Yep."

I thought he was going to grab me again but instead he plucked a damp napkin from a tray and wiped it over his face. The red stain of the makeup transferred to the material, leaving his face unblemished once more.

"Don't forget that pen and paper, Sammy," he said. "Wouldn't want Tristan disappointed now, would we?"

He turned, and for a moment, I got to admire his ass that once again looked damn fine in his jeans. He might be a full-of-himself hockey player but jeez, that was a cute butt and the dark denim just made it all the cuter.

The curtain flicked closed and I spun and sagged against the window, staring down at the dark ocean. What was it about Vadmir that had made me act so unprofessionally? It was as if I couldn't resist. Couldn't say no. I wanted to simultaneously strap him to a bed and fuck him and have him grip me tight and fuck me. And that kiss, wow, that just reminded me of what I'd had... and what had he said about later?

He must be joking, right? There was no later for us.

I reached for my purse, delved inside for my lipstick and compact and set about repairing the damage to my mouth. I had a bee-stung look going on. It seemed Vadmir only did things hard and fast, including kissing, not that I was complaining.

Within a few minutes I'd composed myself. I had a glass of water, smoothed my hair and got my aroused body under control.

I stepped out of the galley and into the cabin. The lights were dim, most of the passengers sleeping or engrossed in movies. A few had overhead lights on that shone down in laser-straight beams onto their books. I handed out warm napkins, like the one Vadmir had helped himself to, and the majority of passengers took the opportunity to refresh.

When I reached Vadmir I set a pen and paper down on his tray without saying a word.

Two minutes later, just as I'd finished folding the used napkins, the call bell pinged quietly.

It was my Russian boy.

I brushed a few bits of fluff from my arms, the napkins had a habit of shedding, and went to him.

"What can I help you with, sir?" I asked curtly.

"Lots of things that I can't tell you about up here," he said, with a maddeningly cute, bad-boy grin.

I sighed. "Have you done the autograph?"

"Yep." He wafted it in the air between us.

I reached for it.

"Ah, ah," he said, not releasing the scrap of paper. "You have to take this first."

"What is it?"

With one hand he folded another piece of paper in half. "It's the name of the hotel I'm staying in tonight. Tomorrow I drive north, to see my family, but I have an early meeting in Moscow with my agent." He paused and a hint of what I thought was vulnerability crossed over his eyes. "I'd like to see you again, Sammy, tonight."

"You mean you'd like to..." I stopped myself saying anything more. I didn't want to incriminate myself further.

"Yes," he said, with a grin. "I would like to see you for that, but also for a beer and to watch the game." He paused. "There's a sports bar in the hotel and the NHL highlights will be on. Meet me there."

"I can't."

"Why not?"

"Because..." I struggled to find an excuse even though I needed one. It was ridiculous what he was suggesting. I couldn't head off across Moscow looking for some random hotel with a sports bar. I was flying out again within twelve hours of landing. It was out of the question.

"Please, Sammy."

"No. What we had was a one-night thing."

He passed me the autographed piece of paper and turned down his mouth. He gave a resigned shrug and his shoulders sagged. "Okay, can't blame a guy for trying, though."

I put both pieces of paper into my pocket and straightened. "Anything else...sir?"

He shook his head and reached for his earphones. "No, that will be all."

Chapter Seven

Staring up at the Grand Hotel on Tverskaya Street in central Moscow, I tried to calm the quiver in my belly.

What was I doing here?

This was crazy of the highest degree.

But for some reason I didn't care. I'd been compelled to come here. I just couldn't settle in my airport hotel room or face an evening of mediocre food and the company of my fellow stewards.

I needed more.

Much more.

I stepped away from the cab I'd just ridden and onto the gritty, damp pavement. The arctic wind nipped at my cheeks and tossed my hair over my shoulders as I hurried forward. My coat wasn't quite thick enough for the sub-zero temperatures. Plus, I was tired and I always felt the cold when I was running on a low battery.

A doorman in a smart burgundy jacket and a beige peaked hat ushered me in with a smile and a semi-bow. He clearly felt sorry for the fact I had no hat and gloves like my fellow pedestrians.

Stepping past him, I was grateful for the warmth of the lobby. I paused to wipe my feet on a large mat that had a golden-colored crest embroidered on its surface. Quickly I reached into my purse, grabbed my Nokia and flicked it to silent. I didn't want to be disturbed. An evening off from constant text chatter with the girls and social media updates was very appealing, especially since I had other items on my agenda.

The low hum of gentle classical music filled the huge area and danced around enormous pillars that supported an ornate ceiling. Large urns of flowers were dotted about, decedent and rich in color their heady scent perfumed the air.

I tightened my purse over my shoulder and walked toward what looked like a bar. The door was half-open and a plush, emerald green carpet with brass trim circled the entrance. It appeared dark and atmospheric inside.

I peeked through the doorway. Not a bar but a restaurant. A very elegant one with white linen tablecloths, candles and a hushed atmosphere.

Hoping I hadn't got it all wrong, I circled the lobby. The Grand Hotel didn't seem the type of place to have a sports bar and I wondered if Vadmir had made a mistake.

Perhaps he was just messing with me?

A receptionist looked up from her computer screen and smiled. I decided to take the plunge and ask her where I might watch hockey. My Russian was incredibly limited but I'd start out polite.

"*Privet*," I said, placing my hand on the walnut desk between us.

Her smile broadened and she nodded, her neat, black bob swaying by her ears. "Good evening, madam, what can I help you with?"

I held in a sigh, was it really that obvious that I was a foreigner? I guessed it was.

"I'm looking for the sports bar," I said, "I'm meeting a friend but I fear he may have been mistaken in the address."

"No, not at all. If you follow this corridor 'round the back of the hotel you'll find the *Hero Bar*. It overlooks the outdoor pool which, in case you were thinking of a dip, is currently out of season."

"Yes, I'm sure it is." I glanced in the direction she was pointing. "And thank you, I'll find it."

"Have a nice evening."

I wandered off, my heeled boots clacking on the floor. An elderly couple, arms linked, walked past me. She was talking in Russian and wore a simple, but beautiful floor-length black dress. He held his head high, as though proud to have her on his arm, and held what looked like tickets in his hand. Perhaps they were off to the Bolshoi later. I wondered what was showing. I'd been once, a few months ago. Harmony and I had sacrificed sleep to enjoy a wonderful performance of *Giselle*.

Ballet wasn't really my thing but the magic had captivated me, whisking me off into a fantastical fairytale world of passion and loss, ghostly figures and love stronger than death.

Continuing along the corridor, I admired the artwork. Austere and stern portraits in heavy, golden frames glared down at me. Unfamiliar landscapes and architecture, all appearing to be originals and protected by glass.

On rounding the corner, a faint scent of chlorine told me there must be a spa nearby with a pool; how nice a sauna would be to warm my bones and soothe my work weary limbs.

The rumbling sound of a commentator reached me at the same time as I spotted the entrance to *Hero Bar*.

So Vadmir had been right.

But was he here?

I stepped in, my feet quieting on the carpeted floor. The lights were dim, the place lit mainly by a big screen and spots behind a long, sleek bar. It wasn't your usual spit and sawdust place. This was one screamed class and sophistication.

The booths around the edge were about half full and a couple of guys sat at the bar. To my right a pool table stood set up, the neatly arranged balls waiting to be fractured apart.

As my eyes adjusted I studied the screen. Hockey was playing, or rather war on ice. A tussle had broken out, gloves were flying off and sticks spinning outward from what looked like a full on fight. I noticed a helmet roll away as a couple of players bashed against the Plexi and one fell to the floor.

The commentary, in Russian, was excitable and fast. I couldn't pick up any of the words, the jabbering one long string of sounds. Eventually a linesman broke two players apart, almost falling himself, and a referee whizzed over, blowing his whistle.

I unbuttoned my coat, warmer from my walk through the hotel and searched for Vadmir. He was so big he shouldn't be hard to find. If he was here, that was.

The commentary stopped and in its place an advert with a high-pitched jingle sang around the room.

My gaze fell on Vadmir. He was sitting alone in the booth farthest from the screen. He had his cap on, as usual, and was staring out of the window into the darkness.

I paused, making the most of seeing him before he saw me. It was an unguarded moment that had my breath hitching. He really was beautiful in a rugged, tough-as-nails kind of a way.

Apparently lost in thought he removed his hat, rubbed the flat of his hand over his hair and then pinched the bridge of his nose. He shut his eyes, screwing them up tight, and pressed his lips together.

A shard of guilt shot through me. I shouldn't be observing him like this, without him knowing. It wasn't fair. I should go to him and make my presence known.

But something held me back. Vadmir was a man of strength and passion yet here, seeing him alone like this with a pained expression, I was reminded of the vulnerability I'd seen earlier.

What was he worrying about? It wasn't whether or not I'd turn up, surely? Did he have more going on in his life? Perhaps it was something to do with the Vipers? Were they losing? And why was he here and not in Orlando playing for his team?

I found myself drawn to him and, before I knew it, I was standing at the end of his table not really remembering walking there.

He opened his eyes and the hand that had been squeezing his nose reached for his beer.

He saw me and stopped with his fingers wrapped around the bottle. "You came?" he said, his lips losing that stern, worried tension of moments ago.

"Yes."

He treated me to a full-on smile that filled me with a honeyed glow. "I am glad," he said.

His full attention did strange things to my knees, chest and everywhere in between. Quickly I sat opposite him, glad to be off my feet.

"You won't be able to see from there," he said.

"See what?"

He smiled. "The game."

"Oh, that's okay."

"No it isn't. We're having a beer and watching the game, that was the deal."

"The deal?"

"Deal, date, whatever you want to call it."

"I don't have a beer."

He held up his hand and called over to the bar, "*Yeshche piva*." He then looked back at me. "It's on its way."

"Thank you."

"Sit next to me. I'll explain what is happening."

I sighed and stood, but it wasn't really a hardship to sit next to him and as his cologne seeped into my nostrils my beer arrived.

"So who is winning?" I asked, sipping the malty drink.

"Penguins, it is not a good game and it doesn't end well."

Maybe that was why he'd been looking so fed up? This was a rerun, he'd obviously found out the final score already. "Was there a fight a few minutes ago?"

"Yeah, Brick got into a ruck with a Penguin defenseman. He's in the penalty box now for two minutes."

"That's not long."

"Long enough for the opposition to score, which is what happens next. Cute wrist flick apparently but damn, Jackson should have stopped it."

"Ah, Jackson," I said. "Perhaps he's tired after his night with Harmony. Not up to the job today."

He laughed and his shoulder jostled against mine. "Yeah, I think she probably did drink him alive."

I giggled. "Do you mean *eat* him alive?"

He shrugged, our shoulders touching again. "I don't know, do I?"

"Yes, that's the saying."

He twirled his index finger near his head. "I am still learning all of your...sayings."

"I've noticed."

"There are so many of them and they make no sense."

"They make perfect sense." I paused. "You must have sayings in Russian."

"Yes, of course." He tipped his head. "*Te, kto v ssorakh vstavit', chasto prikhoditsya protirat' krovavyy nos.*"

Oh, I loved the way he spoke in his native tongue. He'd done it last night, too, but then I'd been otherwise engaged. But hearing him now, with his throaty voice and watching his lips move, it set a slow burn of lust simmering inside of me.

"What does that mean?" I managed.

He nodded at the screen. "It means, people who get involved in others' arguments often wipe a bloody nose." He shrugged. "And it's not unknown, particularly in Russia, for a linesman to get an elbow in the ribs or a stick around his ankles. Best to leave two fighting men alone."

"I like it. Tell me another."

He frowned as though concentrating and sipped on his beer. "Mmm, okay. *Tam net nikakogo sposoba dlya dve smerti priyti k vam, no ot odnogo vy nikogda ne budete bezhat'.*"

I smiled and rested my hands on the table. "What does that one mean?"

"There is no way for two deaths to come to you, but from one you will never run away."

"That's true, death and taxes are two things we must all face with certainty."

"Yes." Again he sipped his drink though this time he turned to the dark window. "We all must die."

I followed his gaze. Outside the pool was covered with tarpaulin and a few low lights were set around a statue of a female ballerina performing an arabesque. She held her arms high and her tutu puffed stiffly out behind her.

"Have you eaten?" he asked, turning back to me.

"No, not yet. We were late disembarking and then the trip to the hotel and then here, I—"

"What kind of man am I?" he said, shaking his head. "We should go and find food, or they do burgers here...no, the restaurant is much nicer."

"Well, I don't know, I'm only dressed in jeans and it looked very posh in there." I smiled apologetically. "When you said sports bar I didn't think it would be housed in a five-star hotel."

"I am sorry. I didn't explain it very well to you."

"It's okay."

He reached out and his fingers, cool from holding his drink, slipped over my ear and into my hair. "Sammy," he said quietly and his eyes softening. "There is another Russian saying that is perfect for you."

"I...what is that?" My skin, over my head and down my neck, was tingling. I was becoming lost in his eyes. They were mesmerizing. When he looked at me, with such intensity, I felt like I was the only woman in the world.

"*Malen'kaya iskra mozhet vyzvat' bol'shoy pozhar.*" He stroked down my neck and rested his hand over my left collarbone, the palm flat as though feeling for my heartbeat.

"What does that mean?" I asked, swallowing and studying the way his pale brown eyelashes fanned out, casting small shadows on his cheeks.

He smiled, leant in close and hovered his lips over mine. "A little spark may cause a big fire." He brushed his mouth over mine. "That's what happened to us. One look, one spark and whoosh...inferno."

"Yes...inferno."

"I saw you, in the parking lot," he murmured. "All sexy and cute with your fluffy hair and red lips."

"You liked what you saw then?" Of course he had. He couldn't have hidden it if he'd wanted to.

"Hell yes and that was some spark, a nuclear spark."

I smiled. "I agree. Nuclear." My nipples were straining against my bra. I was having to force myself not to squirm. Damn, I wanted him again. I wanted that raging furnace of lust to pour into my veins and be matched by his. "Russian boy," I said, resting my hand on his thigh and sliding it upward, toward his groin.

"Yes?"

"I think we should get room service. Forget the restaurant or grabbing a burger."

His nostrils flared and he tugged on his bottom lip with his teeth. "Are you sure?"

"Yes, let's go light some big fires." I skimmed my hand higher, to the interesting creases and tempting bulges in his jeans.

"I'm glad this table is here," he said, shutting his eyes.

I explored and found the length of his cock through the material. He was heading toward full hardness. "Yes, I guess it wouldn't be right for a superstar hockey player to be getting felt up in public."

"So far no one here has recognized me." He paused and blew out a breath as I found the root of his shaft and gave a firm squeeze. "But..." he went on. "Hockey players are not exactly known for good behavior."

"I can agree with that."

"So maybe no one would be shocked."

"Maybe not."

He shifted a little and I cupped his balls. They were packed tight against the seam of his pants and I tickled my fingernails over them. Scratching the denim and sending vibrations through the fabric.

"Ah, *yebat*," he muttered. "I've been thinking about you as I've traveled half way 'round the world. Nothing but you and what you do to me... so be careful or I might embarrass myself here."

"Wouldn't that be fun." I grinned and moved closer, so close I could feel his breath on my face.

"No, I think..." He spoke onto my mouth, his lips moving against mine and the taste of beer intensifying. "I think...it could be damn uncomfortable and really fucking embarrassing."

"So shall we get out of here?"

"Yes."

I tried to stand but he wrapped his arm around my waist and held me against him.

"Sammy."

"What?"

"You really are something else, you know that?"

"What, because I can resist you?" I asked.

"You can?" He raised his eyebrows.

"On the plane." I frowned. "I did then."

"Ah...okay." He tugged me closer, so our chests touched. "I meant that you're beautiful and sassy and so fucking sexy." A small muscle flexed in his cheek. "I don't take women for granted, you know? I am very privileged that you came here tonight. I didn't think you would."

"You asked me to."

"Mmm, but I could tell you didn't want to."

"I did, it's just..."

"What?"

I hesitated. "It's a long way across the city. I'll have to leave in a few hours. Plus, cabs here are extortionate."

"So if I'd been in an airport hotel you would have said yes straight away?"

I hesitated, unsure of the answer, then decided to keep him guessing. "I suppose that's for me to know and for you to find out." I disentangled myself from his grip and stood.

He gulped down the last of his beer then darted out his tongue to swipe it over his top lip.

"Come on," I said, crooking my finger. "We don't have long."

"Long enough." He slapped his cap on and stood. "Long enough, Sammy."

Chapter Eight

"Don't rip it," I squealed, batting Vadmir's hands away from the base of my cashmere sweater. "It's Miu Miu."

"So remove it...fast," he growled, towering over me with a predatory look in his eyes. "Or it will go the same way as your little panties did."

His dark expression did sinful things to the bad girl in me and I wanted more, more of his carnal cravings, more of his dirty desires.

With hurried movements I tugged the sweater over my head. "Yes, you owe me new underwear," I said, panting. "I haven't forgotten."

"Yeah, tomorrow, I'll buy you more tomorrow." He ducked and nuzzled his face into my cleavage, pressing his palms over the outer edges of my breasts to hold them high and together.

"*Yebat'*, you taste good," he murmured, swiping his tongue over the lacy cups of my bra and then suckling my nipples through the fabric. "So good."

I moaned and clutched his head. The urgent, desperate heat of his sucking had my spine weakening.

But I wanted flesh on flesh, so I grabbled at his long-sleeved top, pulling it up his back and trying to drag it over his head.

He paused in what he was doing and finished the job for me. Tossing the top to the floor of his hotel room.

I cupped his pectoral muscles in my hands, leaned forward and laved my tongue over his nipples.

He groaned and slotted his hands into my hair, fisting it in his big hands. "I want it all," he said hoarsely. "All of you."

"You're going to get it," I said, taking his right nipple between my teeth and giving it a teasing bite. At the same time, I squeezed his left with my thumb and index finger.

He jerked. "Ah, yeah, you're making me on fire for you, fuck...Sammy..."

I delved downward and slipped my hand between his flat belly and the waistband of his jeans. His cock was hard and proud and straining upward, the tip escaping his briefs. Eagerly I channeled my finger through his slit, spreading the drop of moisture I found there.

"Touch me all over, Sammy," he said, his breath breezing over my hair. "The way I'm going to touch you. I want to be inside every bit of you."

I trailed kisses down his chest, the base of his ribs and poked my tongue into his navel. I then gave the tiny rise of flesh before his jeans another bite.

"Little minx," he gasped.

"Lose these," I said, popping open the button on his fly. "Now, before I rip them."

As he shoved the jeans and briefs away I folded to my knees. "Fuck my mouth," I said, looking up at him, batting my eyelashes and licking my lips. "Fuck my mouth until you come."

He gritted his teeth, his eyes flashed and he took my jaw in his palm. "Can you take it?"

"Yes, all of it."

He squeezed my cheeks, forcing my mouth wide. "Open up."

I let my jaw hang slackly, only inches from his erection. My mouth was watering, saliva already pooling on my tongue. We'd done many things the night before, but apart from that one brief suck on his cock I had yet to taste him and I loved giving head, adored having an eager cock in my mouth.

He eased forward and the tip slid between my lips. Warm and smooth, his aroused, salty flavor seeped onto my palate.

I moved backward a little, so my shoulders were supported by the wall and gripped his hips to steady myself.

"More," he said, "can you take more...?"

I nodded, his dick moving within my mouth.

He pressed in farther and I wrapped one hand around the section of his shaft that I wasn't accommodating orally.

He moaned and a tremble traveled through his body.

I shut my eyes, loving the warm density of his cock. His veins were throbbing at the surface, pulsating against the roof of my mouth.

I coiled my tongue around his cock and eased him in deeper. He took the hint and slid right to the back of my throat.

For a second my gag reflex nearly overwhelmed me, but I beat it down and pulled in air through my nose. I could feel him lodged there, so far down, and I swallowed, the action pulling on the tiny bit of slack skin at the end of his dick.

"Ah, that's it, fuck me, so good, *dah, dah*," he said, banging one hand onto the wall above me and the other curling around to the nape of my neck.

He set up a thrusting motion with his hips, shoving in and out of me and holding me still. It wasn't a gentle rhythm, it was rough and tough and I struggled to take it. But I would and I could. Saliva dripped from my chin, my breaths were noisy and ragged. I loved it, I loved that he didn't treat me like I might break. I loved how he held me so firm and took what he wanted the way I did with him.

"That is enough..." he said, suddenly pulling out. "I want to be inside you, properly. I want you to come with me."

I sucked in air and dragged the back of my hand over my chin to collect the moisture. But as soon as I'd done that I was standing again. He'd pulled me up, his hands beneath my arms, and plonked me onto my feet.

"Like this," he said, spinning me round. "Against the wall, Sammy. You know you'll love it."

"Condom." I gasped as he dragged down my jeans and yanked my boots off in wild, pitching movements. "Condom, Vadmir."

"Fuck." He left me for a moment and I stepped out of my jeans, then my panties. I was pleased they weren't going to bite the dust like the previous pair.

"If we'd had a bit of privacy on that damn plane," he said breathlessly, "This is what I'd have done to you." He pressed his chest into my back and forced me against the wall, my right cheek squashing on the cool paintwork. "I'd have taken you from behind as you looked out the window at the earth far below. We'd have joined the high miles club as I ground into you hard, so fucking hard..." As he'd spoken the last two words he'd found my entrance with the tip of his cock and pushed in an inch.

"Ah, ah, please, Vadmir," I gasped, parting my legs and shoving my ass into him. I arched my spine, giving him better access.

"It is good, yes?"

"Yes, good, fuck, give me all of you." I was so wet for him, normally this position required foreplay or lube but damn, I was dripping; dripping and desperate for his whole length to bury deep.

"Here it is."

I shut my eyes and gave over to sensation.

He rammed in, trapping me between his body and the wall. I felt weak. I wanted to focus on nothing but him driving into me. I couldn't concentrate on keeping my limbs functioning. But it didn't matter, because again he had me. I was encased in his arms, impaled on his cock. His wide thighs were behind my legs, blocking me in, bracing me tight.

The sound of his belly slapping against my ass cheeks clapped around the room. The heated scent of our arousal swirled and puffed between our bodies with each thrust.

My pussy was clasping and aching. The sweet soreness of his big cock stretching me wide and pounding against my G-spot was bliss.

I clawed at the wall and gasped his name, "Vadmir..."

He smacked his hands over mine, and our fingers interlaced. "Can you come like this?" he asked breathlessly against my ear.

"Yes, yes, it's just right, so deep..." And it was. A glorious G-spot orgasm was tearing toward me. Deep and satisfying, the pressure was building. He was getting it just right. "Don't stop..."

He didn't. He kept on going. For a moment I felt like I needed to pee and then the feeling passed and I toppled over the edge and let my orgasm consume me.

Still he pounded on. As I cried out, he held me tight and drove me ever upwards. My pussy spasmed around him. My whole pelvis was contracting and releasing.

"Come, come with me..." I wailed.

But he didn't. He just continued to surge his thick cock into me over and over. He was so near, moments away. I could tell, by his breaths, and the absolute solidness of his cock.

Eventually he slowed and my orgasm faded. I was panting hard, enjoying the final pulses of my climax that seemed to gather all the muscles in my pelvis and drag them together.

"You didn't..." I gasped.

"Sammy, the night is young." He pulled out and wrapped me in his arms, holding my back into his chest.

I sagged against him. My bra, still in place, was pressing on his forearm. I felt boneless. Vadmir had a way of wringing an orgasm from me that left me one hundred percent sated. My knees gave way. "Oh..."

"Shh..." he said, spreading kisses down my neck and onto my shoulder. "I've got you."

I managed a meek nod.

"Rest," he said, "and then you'll be ready to go again."

I wasn't convinced, but rest sounded like a great idea.

He steered me to the bed and we lay down, in the same position we'd been standing. His thick cock was nestled between my ass cheeks—greedy, hungry but also patient.

I sighed as he continued to gently drop sweet kisses onto my neck, my shoulder and into my nape. They were delicate little touches of his lips, so different to his actions of moments ago. He'd shifted from a wild storm of passion to a peaceful calm. No wonder I was dizzy.

My thoughts fudged as a pleasant doze washed over me. The mattress was so soft, like marshmallow, and I was sinking lower. A dreamy state harnessed my thoughts as Vadmir stroked and caressed me into a slumber.

He pulled away for a moment and then slotted back in, palming my ass cheeks. "Hey, Sammy," he whispered, "are you awake?"

"Mmm," I said, half twisting to receive a kiss.

"You've still got energy, right?" His breaths were hot on my cheek.

"Yes, what's an eighteen-hour flight? Not tiring at all."

He released my bra and pushed it down my arm so I could wriggle out of it.

"You want to sleep?" he asked.

"Hell no. You haven't had your fun yet, Russian boy. Sleep is not on the agenda until that happens."

I felt him smile against my shoulder, his cheek bunching on my skin. "Yes, ma'am."

"How do you want to come?" I asked, wondering if he wanted my breasts again. He'd enjoyed that the previous evening.

"Well..." he said, tweaking my nipples. "You really want to know?"

"Yes, of course."

He slid his hands down my belly, over my navel and then fluffed through my pubic hair. "I love your pussy," he said, just touching my clit.

I murmured as renewed interest captured my nerve endings.

"It's hot and tight," he said, "and hugs me like a perfect winter glove." He smoothed his touch over my hip. "But...this is what I want now." He explored over my left buttock, down my cleft and settled his finger over my anus.

I jerked at the intimate touch.

"Shh," he said. "Here, this is where I want you, but only if that works for you, too."

Oh, fuck, it had been a while since I'd indulged in anal sex. I wasn't averse to it. I just usually reserved it for guys I was in a relationship with, not a one-night stand, or in this case a two-night stand.

"Fuck, you're so sexy, everything about you," he whispered. "I don't know why but I feel so possessive, like I want to own you, claim you. I want you as mine."

I stiffened as he rubbed tiny circles over my asshole. His words, his actions, it was making my body tingle and my mind race.

"Not in a weird kidnap way," he went on, "but in a protect you, make you happy and keep you satisfied way."

"I think you're doing a pretty good job of the satisfied part."

"I'm pleased to hear it."

We were quiet for a moment. Vadmir teasing the tiny wrinkles of skin on my ass and me just breathing and relaxing into the touch. The longer he did it the more turned on I became.

"Yes," I said, "fuck me there, do it."

"Yes?"

"Yes...please."

His finger left me then returned cool and coated in lube. "I want this pretty ass so bad," he said. "Seeing you in that tight skirt, on the plane, damn, I got hard enough to hammer screws thinking of bending you over and..."

"Nails, hammer nails."

"Whatever the fuck you want hammering, I'm your man. Screws, nails, goddamn tomatoes."

I stifled a giggle but then sucked in a breath when the tip of his finger edged into my dark heat.

"Oh, damn it..." he murmured. "You're so little, I don't know if..."

"It's okay." Fuck, was it? His cock had a formidable girth. "Stretch me."

"Sammy...?"

I shoved my ass down, onto his finger. "Stretch me. Fuck, let's do this." I wanted him to come as hard and furiously as I had earlier. Lose it totally. Be unable to stand, speak, function afterward. "Give me more." Lust was a sudden, potent injection of desperation and desire and it had filled my veins.

He obliged and added another finger. The sweet burn made me gasp as my delicate muscles widened for him and welcomed him in.

"More lube," I said.

He gave my shoulder a small bite, his teeth creating a sharp distraction from what was happening below. "Here," he said, increasing the cold, wetness of his fingers. He dragged in a breath, his chest buffeting mine. "Fuck, I'm going to make this so good for you."

"I know." I felt free, liberated. A cock in my most private hole wasn't something I longed for until the temptation hovered before me, then it was all consuming. It seemed my big, bad Russian hockey player felt the same. "Get inside me," I said, fisting the sheets.

"Wait." He scissored his fingers, extending me wider.

I groaned and rejoiced in the hot-honeyed sensation. It was a promise of what was to come.

He pulled out.

The tip of his cock nudged up against me.

Hurriedly, I shot my hand down to my clit. I found it protruding from its folds; engorged and wet, wanton and needy.

As he eased in, parting the tight sphincter of my anus, I swirled my clit.

"Ah, yeah, fuck, take me," he said, *"prinyat' vse moy chlen."*

I gasped and bore down, embracing his entry. For a moment panic washed over me. Could I take him? He was creeping in higher. Not a wild, frantic entry like when he fucked my pussy, this was slow and controlled but oh, so dense and heavy.

I held my breath and closed my eyes. Fought the war within that was to pull away and escape because I knew once seated he would feel incredible filling me.

Continuing to fret my clit, I harnessed the bliss that was traveling high. The fullness was exquisite, his ride, now he'd eased my asshole wide, was a smooth glide to full depth.

"Yes, yes," I hissed. "That's it."

"Fuck," he said hotly against my ear. "Fuck, you're gripping me like a snare."

"It's good, so good." My hand was working like a dynamo, speeding over my clit. "Come, please, come," I gasped. "With me." The thought of surrendering to climax whilst my ass was so full was both terrifying and luring me closer.

He shifted again, getting higher even though I didn't think that was possible.

I groaned and felt his balls mash against the flesh of my ass. He was completely lodged within me. My hole stretched taut around the thick span of his root.

"Here...let me," he said, reaching around and pressing his fingers over mine as I swirled my clit. "Sammy..."

"Yes, yes..." I said, wanting to buck frantically but also frozen with the bliss of what we were doing.

He took over, jamming his fingers against mine and working my nub into a frenzy. Moisture was gushing from me, coating our fingers. He eased his cock out a little and then slid back in.

"So good..." I managed, twisting my neck and trying to kiss him.

He rested his mouth over my cheek, his damp lips tracing my skin.

Again he eased out, pushed back in.

The first tugs of climax lured me closer. I clenched my pussy which in turn made my ass respond with a spasm.

"Argh, yeah, *dah, dah*..." he moaned. "Fuck it."

He pulled practically out and then rode back in, again his balls bashed into me.

My breaths were hard to catch. I felt so owned, so thoroughly filled by him.

"I'm coming..." he gasped, increasing the speed and pressure on my clit. "Fuck."

"Me too." I screwed up my eyes, let a blinding flash of colors streak through my mind and allowed the compression in my clit and the solidity in my pelvis hold me hostage for a few sweeter than sweet moments.

He grunted then groaned, foreign words spilling from his mouth and echoing into my ear.

I jammed myself backward onto him and pushed down on his hand. "Fucking hell..." I moaned, wanting it all, taking it all.

My asshole spasmed around his cock. I was aware of him pulsing inside me, filling the condom. My sensitive muscles were attentive to every gush and ripple through his shaft.

Another long groan reeled from his chest, grating out of his throat and then he fell still and silent.

I enjoyed a few last circles on my clit and then also calmed. I was sucking in air fast, dizzy from the experience. Damn, I'd never taken it so far, so fast with anyone. It seemed Russian was my flavor.

Chapter Nine

I woke with my nose pressed into Vadmir's chest, the tip of which was being tickled by the small patch of hair at his sternum. He was hot and strong and his legs, twisted with mine, held me close, as did his arms, one beneath me and one over my waist.

My memory couldn't recall the moment between awake and asleep, or him being in me and then not. But what I could remember was the fabulous sex we'd had and the sensation of his cock in my ass.

I clenched my sphincter. Yes, still tender. It hadn't been an erotic dream.

I shifted a little and he tightened his grip on me, pulling me closer.

A thick wedge of flesh poked against my thigh. God, the guy was insatiable. We'd just had an amazing time and he wanted more.

Opening my eyes, I saw that it was still pitch black in the room. We had time for another round of action before I had to dash off to the airport and catch my flight.

Trying to disturb him as little as possible, I twisted within his embrace and fumbled on the bedside table. It took a few seconds to locate a condom. When I did, I quickly opened it with my teeth, spat away the small strip of foil and then sidled up to him again. Taking his shaft in my hand, I smoothly and gently rolled the condom down his erection from tip to root.

Silently congratulating myself on finding such a perfect specimen of a cock to play with, I slid on top of him, legs either side of his hips.

I pressed my belly to his, my tits to his chest and let my pussy kiss the tip of his sheathed cock.

He groaned and I held my breath and ceased all movement. I didn't want him to wake until I had him seated fully.

When he quieted, I maneuvered myself carefully, edging him through the damp folds of my entrance and then taking him in an inch.

"Ah, fuck," he moaned and then raised his hands and grasped my cheeks.

Too late, he was awake.

"Shh…" I said, "just enjoy." I planted a kiss on his mouth.

He accepted the kiss and then whispered, "Are you trying to finish me off?"

"No, just making sure we make the most of our time together."

"Oh yeah." He shoved his body upward, shunting into me in a smooth glide.

I gasped and pushed upright, spreading my hands on his pecs and sitting down fully. Fuck, it felt like he was going to push right out of my throat. He filled me so absolutely in this position.

I groaned and flung my head back then started up a hip-gyrating dance that caught my clit just right.

"One hell of a way to wake up," he groaned, palming my breasts.

"Maybe you're dreaming."

"In that case, I don't ever want to wake up."

I could barely make him out through the shadows of the room, but as I clenched my internal muscles, I saw him arch his neck, thrusting his head back on the pillow. The sharp angle of his chin was evident and the tendons in his neck strained. He groaned in a deliciously long un-restrained way.

I rode him harder, bucking and thrusting. He increased the tension on my breasts, pulling and plucking my nipples. The sharpness of the pinching and twisting tore me higher and I moaned and gasped, work-ing my way to a fast, hard climax.

Beep. Beep. Beep.

A tinny noise rang around the room.

Beep. Beep. Beep.

"What's that?" I asked, not slowing my movements.

"Nothing. Yeah, like that, Sammy, just like that."

Beep. Beep. Beep.

"Yeah, it... is...something," I managed as the insistent noise continued.

"Just my...alarm," he said, shifting his hands from my chest to my hips and encouraging me to speed up. "Yeah, faster, fuck so good."

"Alarm?" Why was his alarm going off in the middle of the night?

"Yeah. Jesus, you're hot, girl."

Beep. Beep. Beep.

"Vadmir, the alarm. What...?"

"My agent. I have a meeting with my agent." He was breathless. "Ignore it. He'll wait."

"What...a meeting with your agent now?"

"No, at ten."

"Ten at night?" What was he on about?

"No..." He bucked his hips and we both groaned. "Ten in the morning."

"But it isn't...."

"Mmm, keep going."

I'd had enough of the noise and I slid off him.

"What the..." he said, grabbling for my hips but missing as I scooted to the edge of the bed. I grabbed his iPhone and tossed it at him. "Turn it off, it's putting me off my stride. And set it for the right time, for God's sake."

He glanced at the illuminated screen, the light catching on the sharp angles of his face. His mouth was open, he was panting.

I slithered back over him and allowed his cock to slip neatly into my pussy as though it was meant to be there.

"Oh, yeah," he groaned. "*ideal'nyy.*"

I tipped my head, bit his nipple and he silenced the annoying beeping. "Have you set it right?"

"It was set right," he said, filling his hands up with my hair and tugging.

"What?" I allowed my clit to scrape on his hard pubic bone and enjoyed the yanking on my scalp.

"It is right. It's nine, nine in the morning. I have to meet my agent in an hour."

I froze. Nausea welled within me but I refused to let it take hold. It couldn't be morning. It was the middle of the night. The room was dark as coal. I'd only dozed, not even been in a proper sleep.

"Sammy, don't stop..." he said, shifting beneath me, his cock riding deep.

"Nine. Fuck." I leapt off him, scooted to the dresser and grabbed my purse. I fumbled for my phone and checked the time. Moisture seeped from my pussy and slicked on my thighs as I saw with dismay that my Nokia was still on silent.

Plus, he was right. It was goddamn nine AM.

"Shit, shit, shit!" I jumped up, ran to the window and pulled the curtains wide. Daylight streamed into the room, rude and unwelcome it proved beyond doubt that it was morning and I had indeed slept in—momentously.

"What is the matter?" Vadmir asked, propping himself up on his elbows. His cock stood rigid and sentinel like and was shiny from my arousal. A sheen of sweat slicked over his chest and the diamond-white light from the window caught over his body.

"What's up?" I shouted, rubbing my forehead and pacing to the bed, then back to the window and staring out at the snow-covered rooftops. How was I going to get out of this one? Damn it. I'd likely lose my job. "What's up?"

"Yeah, what's up?" He was maddingly calm.

"I've missed the flight!" I spun to him, hands on my hips, heat rising on my cheeks as my knees weakened with a shot of adrenaline. "That's what the fuck is up."

"Flight?"

"Yes, you moron, my flight. Work. It left Sheremetyevo Airport at eight and I was supposed to be on it." I paused. "Fucking hell."

"So call them, they're probably waiting for you."

"Jesus, no, it doesn't work like that. They'll have gone, left, flown away without me."

I picked up my phone again and saw that I had several missed calls. "Bloody hell." I scrolled through them, three from Patrick and half a dozen from head office in Orlando.

Vadmir leaned forward and wrapped his hand around my wrist. "Calm down, it will be fine. No one is dead."

"I will be. Damn it. I've left them short on crew and..." My heart sank and I sighed.

"What?"

"I have a week of leave now. I had plans to drive to Miami with Harmony, shop, catch some rays by the pool, and now..." I pointed irritably at the window. "I'm likely going to be stuck in the snow for a few days."

He rubbed his hand up my arm and then leaned forward and kissed my shoulder. "Hey, snow isn't so bad." He stroked his finger over my collarbone and then down to my nipple. "Come back to bed. Make a phone call to your boss in a minute, when you're calmer."

He wrapped his arms around me and pulled me close.

I shoved against him and wiggled free of his grip. "No, don't you realize how much trouble I'm in?" I pointed at his cock. "I can't just push this to one side and fuck you. I have to sort this out...now."

He looked hurt and wrapped his hand around his shaft. "So this is going to waste?"

"Yes, I've got more important things to worry about than your damn hard-on."

"Thirty seconds ago you didn't."

"Well everything's changed now."

He snapped off the condom and tossed it toward a bin. It landed perfect shot. "I guess I'll just have to finish myself off."

"Yeah, you will. But be quiet about it." I needed to make that call to head office as soon as possible. The longer I left it the more shit I'd be in. Might as well just 'fess up quickly to my mistake and hope the fall-out wouldn't be too horrendous.

Vadmir stood. "I'll shower. Get out of your way."

I glanced up at him and for a moment I wavered. Damn the man was beautiful. All roped muscle and corded tendons. I adored his pale skin and the way his blond body hair coated his chest and thickened beneath his navel. His crew-cut and angled face gave him an exotic look that hit my buttons and made my pussy clench.

"Feel free to order breakfast, coffee. Whatever. Put it on the room," he said as he strode toward the bathroom. His taut butt swaggered with the confidence and ease of a man who had to be no place fast. People clearly waited for him.

I quashed down that feeling of lust and pulled on my underwear. Much as I had to make this phone call, I couldn't quite bring myself to do it in the nude.

Headquarters answered on the fifth ring but I wasn't surprised, it would be skeleton staff at midnight.

"Hello," I said, "this is Samantha Headington, I'm just touching base because I've missed my flight."

"Samantha, Christ, you've had us all so worried."

Phew, it was Nicola, she was one of the senior supervisors and always friendly and fair. I sent a quick thank you heavenwards that she was on duty tonight. "I'm really sorry. I just can't believe this has happened."

"Are you okay?"

"Yes, fine. I just feel terrible."

"Where are you?" She paused. "Well...I'm guessing Moscow."

"Yes, in the city. I came to visit a...a friend and ended up staying. I overslept. It's as simple and stupid as that and I can't apologize enough."

"Hey, no worries, these things happen. As long as you're okay. You had everyone in a tail-spin looking for you."

My eyes stung a little. She was being so nice, too nice. I didn't deserve it. "I'm so sorry. My cell was on silent. So silly of me."

"Hey, it's okay."

I was silent as I held in a sob.

"I hope you had a nice time with your friend," she said gently.

"Yes, but..." I dropped my head, stared at my pink polished toenails. "I was supposed to be on leave for a week after this return international. I'd made plans with Harmony. And now I feel doubly terrible."

"I spoke to her several hours ago. She's still laid up with food poisoning. She's not going anywhere for a few days at least. Company policy, she can't handle meals."

"Oh, no. I must call her. Poor Harmony."

"Yep, she won't be eating shrimp with hockey players again, that's for sure. What the hell was she thinking?"

"Mmm. Dunno."

"So..." She paused. "I'm looking now. The earliest we can get you back to Orlando on a deadhead is..."

I held my breath. "I don't need a fancy seat, one in the village will do."

"Mmm..." Nicola said. "Struggling here."

"I can work my way back. I'm happy to throw in an extra shift, doesn't need to be a deadhead."

"No, your opposite crew is fully staffed, you'll have to take a seat."

Fuck.

"I can't see anything for the next five flights." She hesitated. "Yes, that could work, six days, the nineteenth, and it's premium class."

"What? Really? By the time I get back my week vacation will be over."

"I'm so sorry, Samantha." She sounded it, too.

Much as I wanted to have a hissy fit about the loss of annual leave I knew it was all my own doing. "Are you sure there's nothing sooner?"

"No, not unless you're willing to pay."

I groaned and thought about the money I'd saved for shopping and my new lease and my already swollen credit card balance. I couldn't justify spending the cash or increasing my debt.

"I'm really sorry," Nicola said again. "Of course you can use the room in the airport hotel for the week. We've got plenty on reserve there, I'll sign it off for you."

"Thanks." I tried to sound appreciative. And I was. The last thing I needed right now was a hotel bill added to the equation. "Can you let Patrick know I'm okay? I'll call him later, when he's landed."

"Sure, I'll get a message to the flight."

"Thanks...and I'm sorry, really I am."

"Samantha, chill out. You've been an exemplary employee for over six years. You're one of our most experienced and valued members of the team, you are allowed to slip up on occasion. No one is perfect."

Again I felt my eyes sting. "Thanks for being so nice."

"I wish I could get you back sooner. If anything changes I'll call."

"Okay."

"So go now and click your phone off silent, for God's sake."

I laughed, but without humor. "Yeah, I will."

"Your ticket will be at the desk on the nineteenth."

"Perfect."

"And find something nice to do. Moscow is a great city, full of culture. Catch a ballet or visit a museum."

"I might just do that."

Nicola hung up and I tossed my phone onto the pillow, stood and walked to the window.

I could hear the shower blasting in the bathroom and the scent of shower gel, woody and strong, drifted toward me. I stared at the higgledy-piggledy tiled rooftops. They were aching with the weight of a new fall of snow. Crystalized sparkles caught the weak sun, winking at me as I scanned the unfamiliar suburban landscape.

Damn it. What the hell was I going to do for a week here?

I spotted a neatly folded toweling robe and pulled it around myself, suddenly feeling chilly. A grunt from the bathroom caught my attention as I yanked the belt into a knot at my waist.

The door was open a fraction and I wandered over and peeked into the steamy room.

The glass shower cubicle was directly in front of me. Through the drip-coated surround I could make out Vadmir standing in the hot, swirling mist. He couldn't see me, his back was turned, one hand flat on the black wall tiles and the other at his groin.

His right shoulder was shifting and the taut muscles of his back rippling. His butt was clenched, the dips at the side enhancing their neat smooth shape. He was rocking, ever so slightly, backward and forward.

I squeezed my lips together, touched the doorframe to steady myself and held my breath.

He was doing exactly what he'd said he do—finishing himself off.

I should go, move. This wasn't for me to watch but I couldn't help myself. I was mesmerized. The sight of him in this private moment totally captivated me.

He grunted again and raised his head to the fall of water. It clung in his short hair, trailed down his nape and into the gutter of his spine in a long, sleek rivulet. I licked my lips, remembering running my tongue up that very section of his body on our first night together.

His speed increased.

I blew out a breath and then pulled it back in, my chest expanding, my heart racing.

"Ahh..." he said, the sound echoing and loud. "Ahh...*dah*."

He came. His knees weakening for a second before he braced them and locked his legs straight. The tense muscles in his back trembled and his butt clenched tighter.

Quickly I stepped away. Guilt at my voyeurism suddenly washing through me. But excitement also tweaked at my nerves. Damn, what a treat to witness a man so comfortable and in total control of his sexual needs pleasuring himself. He couldn't have been that worried about being watched, not if he'd left the door ajar.

Mmm, maybe the day hadn't started out quite so badly after all.

Chapter Ten

Vadmir emerged from the bathroom a few minutes later. He'd wrapped a white towel around his waist and was scrubbing at his hair with another. His cheeks were a little flushed and moisture clung to the center of his chest.

"Did you order coffee?" he asked.

"Yes, and fruit, I hope that's okay."

He smiled. "Yes. Good."

I stood and went to the window again. The sky was bloated with dark gray clouds and fat snowflakes were beginning to fall. The weak sunshine of minutes ago was now a distant memory.

He walked up behind me and wrapped his thick, hot arms around my waist.

I leaned back into him, enjoying the support and strength his body provided.

"How was the call?" he asked quietly against my temple.

I sighed. "They were really nice about it, understanding, but even so I'm stuck here."

"Stuck?"

"Yes, until the nineteenth. Nearly a week."

He pressed a kiss to my head, over my hair, and squeezed me a little closer.

I was surprised at how right the gesture felt. It was the first non-sexual contact we'd had; just a kiss, a touch of lips, an act of comfort.

"So what are you going to do?" he asked.

"I've got a free room at the airport hotel. Not very exciting but I can't exactly sleep on the streets."

"No, not sensible." He lifted his head and I sensed him looking out at the falling snow. "Too cold."

"I guess I'll visit a couple of museums, catch up on a few books I was meaning to read. Just hang out." I paused. "Shame really, I was supposed to be having fun in Miami with Harmony. Sun, sea and shopping."

"And now you have snow instead of sunshine."

"Seems that way."

We were silent for a moment. I watched the snow billowing against the window. Several flakes hit the pane and slid fatly to the sill.

"Come with me," he murmured against my ear.

"What?" I tried to turn but he held me tight, so I was still facing the wintery weather.

"Come with me. I'm going north. After my meeting this morning I'm driving to see my family."

"No, I can't." What a crazy idea.

"Why not?"

"Because you don't want me hanging around when you're with your family." I tutted and shook my head.

"I wouldn't have asked if I didn't."

I twisted within his arms again and this time he allowed me to turn and face him. I looked up into his dazzling blue eyes. There were still a few drips from the shower on his long lashes.

"Really?" I said hesitantly. "But weren't we supposed to be—?"

He grinned. "A one-night stand?"

"Well, yes."

"Fate has thrown us together for longer." He slid his hand up my back, over the top of the thick robe and ran his fingers into my hair. "Say yes, Sammy. It will be fun. I've got some things I must attend to but then I will show you the sights. It is a beautiful part of the country."

"But your family?"

"It will be okay. They moved not long ago. They have plenty of room now. Plus, my sister will adore you. She is obsessed with all things America and will drive you crazy practicing her English on you."

I hesitated and studied his freshly shaven face. He had a tiny cut to the right of his lip.

"I don't know," I said, stepping away and reaching a tissue from the dresser. I dabbed at the cut.

"Why are you not saying yes? It is the perfect solution."

I glanced at my thin coat and my clothes still lying abandoned on the hotel room floor. "I haven't exactly packed for Siberia."

He laughed. "It is *not* Siberia. Heaven help me if I lived there." He shrugged. "And clothes is a minor problem."

I frowned. Clothes were never a minor problem.

"Listen," he said. "If you say you'll come with me I'll organize a new winter wardrobe for you. How does that sound?"

"But why would you do that?" I was disbelieving.

"You don't know?"

I shook my head.

"I like you, Sammy. I want to spend more time with you. And if not having a warm coat and decent boots is the bug in the milk that's stopping you coming with me then I will make it right."

"Bug in the milk?"

His brow furrowed. "Cream... no... ointment. Bug in the ointment."

I grinned. "The fly in the ointment."

"That is what I said." His frown switched to a smile, his eyes sparkling and the hard lines of his jaw softening.

I couldn't deny I liked him, too. More than I thought I would when I'd first met him and his athletic body had pulled me to him like a magnet. But that smile, his gentle giant ways and muddled up sayings were drawing me in.

"Okay, I'll come with you."

His face cracked into an even wider smile. "Great."

"But no fur. I don't wear fur."

"Really?" He looked surprised.

"No. Not my thing."

He suddenly snagged me close, planted a hot, fast kiss on my lips and then said, "Deal, you wait here and I'll have everything you need delivered. We'll leave at noon."

As quickly as he'd grabbed me, he released me.

I felt a little dizzy with the sudden decision and the acceptance of a new "winter wardrobe." I sat heavily on the bed and watched as he dressed, dragged on a huge black coat and then his green cap.

He grabbed a keycard from the side and then stopped with his hand on the door handle.

"What shoe size?"

"Thirty-eight."

"Dress?"

"Four."

He grinned, cheekily, and cupped one hand over his chest. "Here?"

"Seriously?"

"I owe you underwear."

I laughed. "Okay, thirty-two E."

"Got it." He nodded. "Be ready, okay."

Before I could answer he'd gone and I was left staring at the Russian language "Do Not Disturb" sign as it swung left to right on the handle.

I breakfasted on a fruit platter and two cups of black coffee. I'd just surfaced from a deep bubble bath and pulled the robe back around myself when there was a sharp bang on the hotel room door.

"Hang on," I said, twisting a towel around my hair, turban-style and slipping my feet into the complimentary slippers.

I answered the knock and found the pretty female receptionist from yesterday smiling at me.

"Ms Headington," she said, gesturing to a porter standing just behind her. "We have been instructed by Mr. Arefyev to deliver clothing suitable for winter weather."

"Well, er...thank you." I eyed the tall silver trolley the bellhop was holding. It was bulging with a plethora of clothing, the front item looked suspiciously like a long fur coat.

"May I come in?" she asked, stepping in anyway.

"Mmm, yes, do..." I moved aside.

The porter wheeled the clothes in and then retreated.

She spoke to him in Russian and then shut the door, turned to me and smiled again.

"I hope this selection will suit your needs. I'm afraid it was a rather limited time-scale that I was given but I have managed to find all the essentials in your size."

"Thanks." The clothes appeared to be ranked in order of warmest. With the rich-chocolate, furry coat at one end and at the other several tiny bra and panty sets in an assortment of pastel colors and one in rich scarlet.

"This," she said, reaching for the coat. "Is an essential."

"It's very nice of you to do this," I said, pressing my palms together and taking a step back. "But I don't wear fur."

She tipped her head forward, her sleek hair sliding fluid-like to her shoulder. "I am well aware of that, Mr. Arefyev was most specific. But this..." She paused and stroked her hand down the soft lapel. "Is finest quality imitation. No animal has ever been near it." She held it forward. "Feel, it is wonderful."

I eyed it suspiciously. "Are you sure?"

She smiled. "Yes, more and more people are demanding this, it means for excellent products."

I stepped closer and touched the coat. It was so soft if was like touching air, the brown hued-strands barely tickling over my fingers.

"Would you like to try it on?"

"Well, yes, I suppose." It was certainly better than the thin navy coat I'd brought with me on what I'd thought was going to be a very brief overnight stay in Moscow. "But." I hesitated, I was naked beneath the robe.

"Ah," she said, placing the coat on the bed and then reaching for the scarlet bra and panty set. "He said you would need dressing from the bottom up."

"He was right. I have only the clothes I arrived here in last night."

"That is not a problem any longer. Here." She passed me the underwear. "Go, I think you will approve."

I took the hanger and went into the bathroom that still held the scents of the vanilla bubble bath I'd taken.

A label hung from the hanger—Agent Provocateur. Oh, boy, was I a lucky girl. I adored AP lingerie but had only ever owned a few pieces.

Quickly I hung the robe on a hook on the back of the door, and slid into the panties and bra. They fit like a dream, the intricate lace as delicate as silk on my skin and the bra-straps a pretty shade lighter than the cups.

I stuck my head around the door, a smile creeping across my face. "Perfect," I said.

She nodded, as though she knew they would be. "And these." She passed in a pair of black pants and a sweater as red as the underwear.

"Thanks." I took them. Shut the door and checked out the labels. Dior trousers and a Dior sweater. A small bead of sweat popped on my temple. I could guess how much these had cost. I'd admired Dior for many years and had treated myself to a few staple pieces. I slipped the pants on, praying they'd fit.

They did, hugging my curves in all the right places and fitting my waist perfectly. I removed the towel from my head and pulled the sweater on. It fit the same, the material warm and caressing against my skin, almost like wearing a cloud.

I moved from the bathroom and held my hands out, palms up, in a what-do-you-think gesture.

"Yes, very good," she said, smiling. "Now the coat." She held it forward and I slipped my arms in.

"Oh, this is nice." I buttoned it and tightened the belt at my waist. It hit just below my knees and came right up around my neck.

"You like?"

"Oh, yes." I smoothed my hands down it and moved to the full-length mirror. "It's beautiful."

"Indeed. And just what you will need if you are staying in Russia for a few days. It is not sun-bathing weather here."

"Definitely not."

"But there is more," she said. "Boots." She handed me a pair of thick black socks and then rummaged in a box.

I sat on the edge of the bed and tugged the socks on. Like everything else they were beautiful quality.

"Here," she said. "You will need these for snow and ice." She held aloft a pair of black boots that had an intricate lace detail holding in the slightly padded exterior. They looked both trendy and practical.

"Oh, I like," I said, reaching for them then putting them on. "And, yes they fit, too." I pushed my damp hair over the collar of the coat. "It all fits so well. How did you manage it?"

"I was given very precise instructions. I was to leave nothing to chance." She straightened, walked toward me and placed a hat on my head.

It matched the coat and when I glanced in the mirror I saw that it was Cossack style.

"These are all the rage at the moment," she said. "And not just in Russia."

A giggle burst up from my chest. "I love it. Really I do."

"You are very easy to dress."

"Well it's not hard with all of this to choose from."

"So you are pleased with my selections?'

"Yes, very."

"Good. I have you something else." From the base of the trolley she pulled a brown leather holdall. "I took the liberty of adding a toiletry case, Clarins, to this luggage bag. I trust that will be okay. If not, I can change it."

"No that's perfect, and thank you."

"It should all fit in here. Would you like me to pack for you?" She gestured toward the rail which still held several jumpers and more pants, plus what looked like a small, black nightdress.

"Pack?"

"Yes."

"All of it?" She must be mistaken. Surely it was just for me to choose from? Pick a selection. I couldn't possibly take all of it.

"Yes, all of it. Unless." She paused and looked worried. "There is something you don't like. I probably have time to exchange it for you."

"No, not at all. It's all beautiful."

I studied the clothes, running my fingers over the hangers and then fingering the material of the short velvety nightdress. Did Vadmir actually mean for me to accept all of these clothes? It was too much. They were all designer, all expensive labels.

"It's so much," I said, more to myself than the receptionist.

"It is what you will need, so I have been told."

"Well yes, but..." I turned to her. "It must have cost a fortune."

She smiled and inclined her head. Her eyes softened, as though some of her professional demeanor had slipped. "If a hockey player is willing to dress you up like his very own doll. I wouldn't complain."

"I...but..." Doll?

She touched my elbow. "Go dry your hair. I'll get this packed up for you. If you're not ready at twelve there will be trouble."

I let her slip the coat from my shoulders and then steer me to the dressing table where I sat. She set a bottle of hair volume spray in front of me and a new roller brush. After fiddling with a plug she placed the dryer in my hand.

Feeling overwhelmed at Vadmir's generosity, I set about teasing my blonde locks into their usual bubbling mane of curls. Seriously, I'd only teased about him buying me new panties, his company that night had been worth the sacrifice. This was so much. Too much.

Chapter Eleven

As Vadmir strode into the hotel room the scent of cool outdoor air breezed in with him. "Ready?" he asked, his movements all business as he grabbed his case from the side and dropped it on the bed.

"Yes." I rose from the chair by the window where I'd been reading a tourist magazine.

"Good. We'll head straight off and grab food on the way." His cheeks were a little red and his cap held watery drips that must have once been snow. The material on the shoulders of his jacket was also wet, the moisture sitting in tiny beads on the surface.

"Where exactly are we going?"

"About four hours north from here, to my home town Sokol, just past Vologda."

"Oh, okay." I'd never heard of either place.

"It is an easy journey," he said, flicking his case open. He disappeared into the bathroom and then reappeared, threw his toiletry bag in and locked it shut. "Snow-plowed freeway the entire trip. We will not need the snow chains."

"Oh, that's good."

He stopped and looked at me. His gaze down the length of my body was like a heated caress. "How are the clothes?"

"Great. I mean perfect. But there were so many. Did you mean for me to have them all? Because really, you shouldn't have. I can't—"

"Shh..." He walked over to me and put his hands on my waist, his fingers almost spanning my torso, spine to belly. "Of course I meant for you to have them all. You can't just have one outfit for a week away or one set of underwear." He grinned. "Though, of course, if I had my way you'd just be naked for the entire time but I think my mother would have something to say about that."

"Your mother?" Suddenly the thought of meeting his mother seemed rather daunting.

"Yes, she's very traditional." He stroked his hands up my back. "I love this sweater, it's so soft and...girly."

I leaned into him, just a little, and let a pleasant shiver wander up my spine. I liked his touch, I'd worry about meeting his mother later. "The receptionist, the woman who came with all of these clothes, she obviously has elegant and expensive taste."

"Yes, I thought she would have." He glanced at the brown leather bag, sitting on the dresser. "So everything is in there?"

"Yes, and my coat is hanging in the wardrobe."

He released me, went to the wardrobe and pulled out my new outdoor wear.

"Mmm, this will be good and warm." He held it open and nodded for me to put it on.

Once buttoned, I reached for the hat, flicked my curls over my shoulders and placed it on so that it covered my ears and touched the fluffy collar at my nape.

"Off we go," he said, managing to hold both bags and pull the door wide for me to go through. "Let's strike the road."

I enjoyed the ride out of Moscow. Vadmir took us in a different direction to the routes I'd used before to and from the airport, and the architecture was both stunning and imposing.

The snow didn't let up, but the BMW 4x4 Vadmir had hired didn't seem to mind, and with the heating turned up and classical music playing on the radio I soon settled into the road trip.

Vadmir pointed out various points of interest, the Moskava River, the Tretyakov Gallery and one of his favorite restaurants that apparently served caviar and pancakes that were the best in the whole of the city.

When we reached the M8 I dropped my hat onto the back seat and stretched out my legs.

"So tell me about your family," I said.

He glanced at me, his eyes soft but also holding a shard of worry. "Things aren't great, that's why I'm here and not playing for the team."

A knot twisted in my belly? Damn, as I'd feared, I would be imposing. "What do you mean?"

"My father's sick. He's always suffered with his chest, *khrupkimi astma*. I think it translates as brittle asthma, but I fear he's very ill this time." He gripped the steering wheel until his knuckles paled.

"I'm sorry to hear that." I paused. "Perhaps you should just drop me at the airport after all, before we go much farther. I'd really hate to be intruding on family time. Especially if someone is sick."

"You won't be. It's fine." He sucked in a deep breath and then blew it out. "I haven't seen them for nearly a year. I'm hoping it won't be any worse than usual. My mother is usually so calm on the phone but when I spoke to her a few days ago there was something about her tone that scared the shit out of me." He paused. "Like she thought the grave was waiting for him."

"So you came straight away?"

"Yes, on the first available flight anyway, which was yours." He smiled but it didn't reach his eyes. "I told my sister to get the doctor to the house again. One from Vologda who specializes in his lung condition. I'm hoping that he will have improved by the time I get there."

"Yes, let's hope so." I twisted my hands in my lap. "I don't know much about asthma but if I can help around the house then I'm happy to."

He reached over, squeezed my knee, then gripped the wheel again as he whizzed past an arctic truck that was kicking up a snowstorm with its huge bulk.

"So how long have you played for the Vipers?" I asked, relieved to get past the truck.

"Four seasons now. I'd admired them for years and they are the only team I would have left my homeland for."

"Really?"

He shrugged. "Of course."

"And did you play in Russia? Professionally?"

"Yes, from the age of nineteen. I've been playing for over ten years now. I'm an old timer in hockey terms."

"What made you get into it?" I gestured outside at the snow-strewn landscape. An endless expanse of white dotted with small, bleak houses that appeared hunched against the brutal weather. "Are there many rinks around or did you play on a lake?"

He laughed. "We have a rink in town, and it was my father's fault. He is a mad fan and before I'd even started kindergarten he had me in skates and with a stick in my hand."

"I bet he's real proud of you now."

He nodded. "Yes, he is. But you'd better watch out, because he has a room full of fan paraphernalia and a million hockey stories that he's happy to tell over and over again." There was a softness to Vadmir's voice as he spoke of his father.

"Do you like this music?" he asked, turning the radio up slightly, his fingers ridiculously big against the small button.

"Yes, it's soothing."

"Sergei Prokofiev, one of my favorite composers of the last century."

I raised my eyebrows in surprise. "You're a fan of classical?"

He laughed. "Don't be so surprised. I might be a brute on the ice but I have a cultured side."

I smiled. "I'm sorry, I didn't mean to... yes, I do like it. It's soothing. I listen to classical when I'm jet lagged and can't sleep. Even if I don't get REM at least my brain has a rest. I find it lulls me into a meditative doze if I pick the right music and I feel refreshed afterward."

"Yes, I know what you mean." He braked hard as a cranky old car pulled out in front of him without indication.

I shifted forward against my safety belt.

"Sorry," he said. "Bad driving is epidemic over here."

I tried not to grip the seat as he undertook and then sped away. The BMW engine swift and strong and easily leaving the other car behind.

"There's a café, about halfway," he said. "We'll stop there for lunch if you can wait that long."

"Yes, that's fine." I sought out my St. Christopher and rubbed it between my thumb and index finger.

Darkness had fallen by the time Vadmir pulled up outside a large apartment block on the outskirts of Sokol. Silvery light from street lamps flooded the parking lot, and I could make out piles of snow stacked up at the corners.

As he rounded the front of the car to open my door I glanced upward.

It appeared much nicer than the other blocks we'd driven past. The outside was painted a warm cream rather than gray and the front entrance had a covered porch supported by pillars. Vadmir had explained that he'd moved his family to this new development a little under a year ago. It had taken him a long time to persuade them to relocate but eventually they had. His sister still lived with his parents, to help look after them, and she worked in a local shop.

"This looks nice," I said, as I took his offered hand and stepped onto the frozen ground.

"Yes, it is. I wanted to buy them a house but they wouldn't have it. Most Russians live in blocks, and my parents always have, it is their comfort zone. But the views are awesome from their penthouse. It was a good choice."

I pulled my coat tighter as Vadmir grabbed our luggage. It had been chilly in Moscow but it was several degrees colder up here toward the Arctic Circle. Plus, the night had crept through the air now, stealing any meager warmth from the day.

"Come," he said, striding forward, shoulders hunched and great puffs of air billowing from his mouth. "This way."

As we rode the elevator a rush of nerves hit me again. I hardly knew Vadmir and here I was about to meet his family. *Stay* with his family. What if they didn't like me? What if I couldn't eat anything? Russian food could be strong on my tastebuds. Perhaps my arrival would make them think there was more to our relationship than there was. We hadn't even been on a date, just screwed each other crazy. We were hardly at meet-the-parents stage.

But I didn't have time to worry about how I'd ended up in this situation, because within seconds we were standing outside apartment thirty-nine and Vadmir was hammering on the door.

It flew open almost immediately and a woman—about my age, with mousy brown hair in a short bob—stood before us.

"Vadmir," she squealed, hurling herself at him. "*Ty zdes'.*"

While still holding the cases, he wrapped one arm around her waist, supporting her body as both her feet lifted off the floor.

"*Eto bylo slishkom dolgo,*" she said.

"It *has* been too long," he said, releasing her. "But please, speak in English. I have company who speaks very little Russian."

"Oh, I am...sorry," she said, turning to me and pressing her hand on her chest. "I didn't understand that."

"It's fine." I smiled, "Don't apologize."

Her face lit further and I saw that she had Vadmir's startling blue eyes along with the same softness to them. "It will do me well to practice English. Are you from America?"

"Yes, Darya, she is," Vadmir said, "I told you that when I called earlier."

"Samantha," I said, holding out my hand. "Pleased to meet you."

Before I knew it she'd clutched my shoulders and planted a kiss on both of my cheeks and then a third on my right cheek. "Come in," she said, "you must be hungry. All the way from Moscow is so far."

We stepped into the large hallway. It was sparsely furnished and Darya took my coat and hung it on a row of pegs next to several warm winter jackets.

"*Vadmir, oh, Vadmir, moy mal'chik, nakonets, zdes'.*" A woman who could only be Vadmir and Darya's mother bustled into the hallway. She wore a blue flowery dress with a black apron over the top. She had a dotty red headscarf wrapped around her head knotted at the nape, and a few strands of gray hair peeked out. Her blue eyes were watery and she had a cross on a chain that sat at her throat.

Vadmir put down the cases and embraced her. His thick arms holding her close and his jacket rustling as they hugged. "*Da, ya zdes' mat'.*"

She pulled away. A tear rolled down her cheek.

Vadmir wiped it away with his thumb. "*Zdorov'ye i ottsa?*"

She shook her head and dipped into the pocket of her apron, pulled out a handkerchief.

"He is no better," Darya answered for her mother. "Not today."

Vadmir frowned. "And what did the doctor say when he visited this time?"

"He hasn't seen him yet. Next week we have an appointment at the hospital."

"Next week?" Vadmir shook his head and his mouth hung open. "What? I thought he'd been to see him twice now."

Darya glanced at her mother. "She wouldn't let me get the specialist in Vologda to come here."

"Why not?" Vadmir shrugged out of his coat and hung it up beside mine. I knew him well enough to know that he was trying to keep sharpness from his voice.

"Money," Darya said.

He clenched and unclenched his fists then turned around. "I told you, Darya, it is not a problem. Spend what you have to spend." He paused. "I also told you one week ago to get the doctor here."

"I know, but..." She gestured to their mother who was studying me. "What can I do when she says no?"

"You just do it, that's what." Vadmir stepped forward and through another doorway. "Where is he?"

"In bed. He's been there for weeks." Darya rushed after Vadmir and I was left alone with their mother.

"*Dobro pozhalovat' v nash dom*," she said, holding out her palms, as if gesturing to the floor of the hallway.

"Hello," I said, smiling and shifting from foot to foot. "Thank you for letting me stay in your lovely home." She had piercing eyes and was nibbling on her bottom lip. I got the impression I was being judged as a potential daughter-in-law. No wonder my legs were a little twitchy, they were in run mode.

She made a cup shape with her hand and tipped it at her mouth. "*Napitok?*"

"Yes, please." I smiled. "That would be great." It had been hours since my last coffee.

"*Dah, dah.*" She nodded and turned.

I followed.

A long corridor with several doors leading off it led to a large kitchen. Like the hallway it was sparse and functional. But the glossy white cabinets appeared high quality and had trendy chrome fittings. There was a multi-burner stove and a large American style refrigerator with water and ice dispenser.

Vadmir's mother reached into a cupboard beside the huge window that held no curtains and pulled out a bottle of vodka and two shot glasses.

She set them on the granite-covered island in the center of the kitchen and poured.

"*Napitok*," she said again.

I walked over, set my purse on a tall, white leather stool and took the offered drink. "Thank you. *Spasibo.*"

She touched the rim of her glass to mine and then drank her vodka in one go.

I watched her lick her thin lips, then studied the clear liquid in my glass. It looked innocent but I knew it would burn like fire.

"Samantha," I said, pointing at my chest and biding for time. We should, after all, swap names.

"*Dah*, Samantha." She nodded and patted her throat, over the cross. "Zoya."

"Zoya."

She smiled and nodded at the drink. "*Napitok*, Samantha."

I glanced at the vodka again, braced and then tipped it into my mouth. It was like a whip had been slashed over my tongue, its cruel end reaching right the way down to my belly. Instantly my eyes moistened and I sucked in air to cool the burn.

As I gasped Zoya reached out and took a lock of my hair in her hands. She pulled it over my shoulder and examined it. It was long, much longer than most people's and I could see that she was interested.

As she spread the strands out between finger and thumb I glanced at the tap, wondering if it would be rude to get water to wash away the taste.

Loud footsteps on the tiled floor alerted me to Vadmir. He went to the cupboard, grabbed a glass and then poured a healthy measure of vodka. He downed it in one go. "I have to make a few phone calls," he said to me, apparently unaffected by the burn. "I'll be right back." He frowned and studied my damp eyes. "Are you okay?'

"The vodka is strong," I said, my voice hoarse. I then glanced at his mother who was still touching my hair. "And..."

"She always wanted to be blonde," he said, tapping his head. "I got this from my father."

"Oh."

"I'll be right back." He pulled his cell from his jeans pocket and left the room. Within seconds I could hear him talking loudly in his native tongue.

"*Mat'*, what are you doing?" Darya appeared, her slippers silent on the floor. "You can not play with guests' hair." She smiled at me in an apologetic way. "I'm sorry."

"It's okay," I said, wishing Vadmir was still in the kitchen.

"And she's given you vodka. I told her Americans like cosmopolitan cocktails."

"Well, yes, but actually, coffee would be great."

"Coffee, yes, yes, I do that now." She touched her mother's hand and shook her head.

Zoya released my hair and poured herself another vodka. She didn't take her gaze from me.

Chapter Twelve

One hour later and I sat alone, in the living area, as the specialist doctor from Vologda examined Vadmir's father. The whole family had gone into the bedroom and shut the door, Vadmir giving me a brief apologetic look as they went.

I'd yet to meet the father, it seemed he was too sick to have a new visitor. If he was this bad I was anticipating a hospital admission. Asthma could be nasty. I'd had a few passengers suffer attacks over the years.

The sofa was a little hard and threadbare and didn't match the beautiful walnut units that filled one wall and housed a plus-sized television. A low, seventies-style table held a pile of hockey monthlies and what looked like a Russian gossip magazine. This room, unlike the kitchen, had curtains covering a huge window; they were a rich chocolate velvet and complemented the cabinets beautifully.

I sipped my coffee and then flicked through the celebrity mag, wondering if I'd recognize anyone.

I didn't.

Finally, there was movement and I heard the doctor leave. The front door shutting and a chain being drawn across it.

I looked up as Vadmir came into the room.

He sat on the arm of the couch, his weight shifting it slightly, and rested his head in his hands.

"How'd it go?" I asked. I had the urge to hold him, comfort him, but I wasn't sure if that was something he'd want.

He twisted his head and looked at me. "The doctor told him to go to hospital, but he's a stubborn fool and refused."

"Oh, that's not good."

"So I've organized for the hospital to come to him. It seemed like the best solution. He needs oxygen, stronger inhalation medicine and nursing care once a day. The doctor said the oxygen will be here first thing in the morning." He shook his head. "It drives me crazy."

"What does?"

"Darya could have done all of this. I told her to, weeks ago."

"Why didn't she?"

"They always worry about the money. I've told them, over and over, we are not poor anymore. We can have what we need, more than we need. I have a good job in America."

He looked so exasperated, so despairing, that I stood and walked over to him. I set my hand between his shoulders and rubbed in slow circular movements.

He sighed and his muscles relaxed a fraction. "But they just won't spend it." He gestured around the room. "I told them, get a new sofa, a big chair so my father can enjoy the view. Rugs on the floor so my mother's arthritic feet are warm, pictures, books, but still they use the furniture from my childhood and live with hardly anything."

"Perhaps they prefer it that way."

"No, they just won't spend the money. Always saving it for a snowy day."

I was sure he'd meant rainy day but snowy did kind of work here, so I decided not to correct him on that one. "The units and television are lovely."

"Yes, they were part of the house when we bought it, anything that doesn't look like it should go to the rubbish heap was on the specification when I filled in the forms." He sighed and put his face back in his hands.

I stepped up closer, so that his head was level with my chest and pulled him into a gentle embrace. I hated seeing him so desolate. It tugged my heartstrings and made my stomach heavy.

He allowed me to pull him close. He didn't cuddle me back, just rested his head on my breasts.

I stroked up his neck, over the back of his head and down again, to his shoulders. Hoping the gesture would be soothing and assure him he had my support, even if I couldn't actually do anything about the situation.

We were silent for a few minutes. The ticking of the clock and our breaths the only sounds in the room. I wondered if he could hear my heart beating.

Eventually he lifted his head and looked up at me. "He's had steroids and antibiotics. He's feeling a little stronger, would you like to meet him?"

"Yes, of course, but only if he's up for it."

"Yes, he is better for me being here apparently." He tutted and skimmed his hands around my waist and up my back. "I wonder if they did this just so I'd come home."

"You don't really think that?"

"I would not put it past them." He stood and released me. "This way."

As we went into the corridor the smell of cooking, something rich and meaty, wafted toward me and my stomach rumbled.

"*Otets eto*, Samantha," Vadmir said, entering a large bedroom painted mossy green and with a double bed in the center.

For some reason I'd expected Vadmir's father to be small and wizened. But he was still a big man. Wide shoulders, broad chest and a sharply angled face, much like his son's. He also still had a full head of white-blond hair.

"*Privet*...Samantha," he said in a weak voice as he hit mute on a remote control.

The commentary of a hockey game was silenced.

"This is my father, Ruslan," Vadmir said.

"Pleased to meet you," I said, "I hope you're feeling better soon."

Ruslan nodded and smiled. He was studying me the same way his wife had.

"He doesn't speak a word of English," Vadmir said. "My mother doesn't, either."

Ruslan held out his hand, gesturing me to go closer.

I walked over and he took my hands in his, turned them over and smoothed his gnarled thumbs over my palms.

"*Ona ochen'...krasivaya, Vadmir.*" He paused and pulled in a breath that looked difficult to reach any depth. "*Vy ochen'...schastlivyy chelovek.*"

"What did he say?" I glanced at Vadmir.

"He thinks you are very beautiful and I am a very lucky man to have you."

"Oh...well...?"

Vadmir laughed. "Don't worry, just because you're here, it doesn't mean you have to marry me."

It was as if he'd read my mind and I grinned and leaned forward, kissed Ruslan on his cheeks, three times, as was the Russian custom.

He smiled and patted my shoulder.

"Back in a minute," Vadmir said, disappearing.

Ruslan gestured around the room, bringing my attention to the vast assortment of hockey collectables. He had shelves of trophies, hooks heavy with medals, a large bowl of pucks and rows of caps hanging from the wall beside the mounted television.

"*Zdes' vy otets,*" Vadmir said, striding into the room again. He placed a black cap with white embroidery on his father's head: New York Rangers.

Ruslan plucked it off and excitement shone in his eyes as he examined a scrawled autograph.

"Todd Carty," Vadmir said. "*Ya poluchil yego dlya vas , kogda my igrali ikh v proshlom mesyatse.*"

He then turned to me. "I got it for him when we played Rangers last month, for his collection."

"Yes, impressive."

"Todd...Carty," Ruslan said, running his finger over the signature. "*Ochen' khorosho.*"

"Todd Carty is the best forward in the NHL," Vadmir said, "and Rangers is one of the few caps missing from my father's collection. He's had all the Viper caps for ages." He pulled a puck from his pocket. "He'll love this, too, it's the puck from the game."

Ruslan's eyes sparkled as Vadmir handed him the small black disk. He turned it over and over in his hands, studying the small Rangers logo in the middle.

Zoya bustled in, tray in her hands. "*On dolzhen yest' vrach skazal.*"

"Yes, he must eat." Vadmir rested his hand in the small of my back. "Come on, so should we."

"Goodnight," I said to Ruslan. "I hope you sleep well and feel better in the morning."

He smiled as the tray was set before him and again his likeness to his son struck me. He, too, would have been an incredibly handsome man in his younger years.

We dined on thick chicken stew that tasted strongly of dill and garlic. Heaps of rye bread came with it and I was pleased to escape more vodka and have water. I felt better after a hearty meal. It had been a long day.

Darya was keen to ask me about Hollywood and New York. Places she longed to visit, and as I told her about my travels with the airline she drank up the details. Her English was good and she clearly had a dose of wanderlust. I knew what that was like; it was why I'd become an air steward, it was a free way to see the world.

"Where did you learn English?" I asked her.

"At night school, ready for when I travel to beautiful places."

"You should come to America for a visit."

"I will one day." She paused. "And also Spain and France, but for now I am busy here, with my parents." She glanced at her mother who was beginning to clear away the plates.

"I am very grateful that you are here, looking after them," Vadmir said to her, leaning back and folding his arms. "It means a lot to me."

"I am happy to do it." She tipped her head and studied him. "But you do need to come home occasionally."

"I am here now."

"Yes." She reached for her water and took a sip. "You are here now."

I glanced between the two of them and wondered if what Vadmir had said earlier was true, about it being an orchestrated plan to get him back to Russia for a visit. There was no doubt about it, Ruslan was sick, but Darya was a perfectly competent individual and I'm sure she could have handled her parents with Vadmir's support.

A sudden wave of tiredness washed over me. I pressed my hand to my mouth and stifled a yawn. "Oh, excuse me," I said.

"I should show you to your room," Vadmir said, "get your bag for you."

"I think so. I'm ready for bed."

Darya smiled and stood, gathering the last of the plates. "Goodnight, Samantha."

"Would you like help to wash up?"

"No, it is okay. We will do it."

"Are you sure?"

"Yes, please, we are happy to have you here."

"Thank you." I paused. "Goodnight, Zoya."

Zoya walked over to me and took my hand. She then led me from the kitchen and down the corridor in the opposite direction of the front door. We went past several rooms including Ruslan's and then she stopped at the end one. A white door that was slightly ajar.

"Samantha," she said, pointing into the room.

"Yes, thank you." I smiled.

She turned, pointed to the last door we'd passed. "Vadmir." Her voice was stern and then she reached for my left hand and tapped my ring finger, over the knuckle. "*Net svad'by ne krovat'*."

Vadmir walked toward us carrying my holdall. He was shaking his head and smiling. "What did she say?" I asked.

"No ring, no sharing a bed." He shrugged and tipped his head backwards. "That is my room and this yours."

"Oh, okay." I'd presumed we'd share a room. The last twice I'd been in bed Vadmir had been with me. But he'd mentioned in the car about his mother being very traditional.

"Sorry," he said.

"Don't be. I'm tired."

Zoya reached up and planted three kisses on my cheeks and then patted my arm. She wandered back to the kitchen.

"Come," Vadmir said. "This is the guest room. I'm not sure if it has ever been used."

He flicked on the light and we walked in. Like the rest of the apartment it was nicely decorated with thick red curtains and bedding to match. There was a fitted wardrobe with chrome handles and a large mirror on the wall. Apart from that it was sparse.

"It has an en suite," Vadmir said, opening a small door that I hadn't noticed.

"Oh, that's useful."

He placed my bag on the end of the bed. "And there are spare blankets in the cupboard if you're cold, or there were last time I was here." He pulled open the doors and nodded. "Yes."

"I'll be fine. It's nice and warm indoors."

"Yes, this block has very good insulation, one of the reasons I moved them here."

"It was very kind of you." I dropped my purse next to the holdall. "Everything that you do for them. You're a good son."

"I'm glad that you think so, but I do feel guilty."

"Why?"

"For being so far away."

"These things can't always be helped."

He stepped up to me, close, so that his chest was right in front of my face. "Sammy," he said. "I'm glad you came to Sokol with me."

Looking up, I breathed in his cologne and felt his body heat radiate toward me. "I'm glad you asked me."

He smiled. "That's sweet of you to say but it has not been much of a vacation for you so far." He slotted his hand into my hair, his palm sliding over my ear. "I'll make it up to you tomorrow."

"Okay," I whispered, resting my hand at the top of his chest, on the first rise of the ball of his shoulder.

"I'll take you," he said quietly and leaning down so his lips were a hairsbreadth from mine. "To the forest, it is beautiful." He brushed his mouth over my top lip. "Just like you."

I fluttered my eyes shut and leaned into him.

He kissed me, softly, sweetly. The frantic passion, the mating of mouths—tongues wild, teeth clashing—of the previous times we'd shared kisses had gone. This was a delicate whisper of a kiss that gave me the chance to feel the shape of his lips against mine. No rushing or gasping, just appreciating the tempo of a seductively sexy kiss.

I sighed and wrapped my arms around his neck. He drew me closer, one palm in the small of my back, the other slipping to my nape and cradling my skull.

He slanted his head, the kiss deepened. His warm tongue stroking mine and the heat from his breaths warming my cheek.

A tremor tickled my pussy and my nipples tightened against the inside of my fancy new bra. Suddenly the separate room thing didn't seem such a good idea. Perhaps we should just roll into bed and get naked the way we usually did.

"Damn, you're a temptation," he said, pulling back and licking his lips. "And I don't think I can resist." His eyes glinted with sudden mischief and he dropped his hand to my ass and gave it a lingering stroke.

"Vadmir."

A sharp voice at the doorway caused us both to turn.

Zoya stood there, hands on hips and her brow creased.

Vadmir snapped his palm off my butt cheek.

"I think you'll have to resist," I said, quickly stepping away from him. Though as I did I missed his body against mine. The solidity and strength of him and the way he'd just held me so gently was intoxicating.

"Seems that way." His surprised expression turned into a grin and he took my hand, kissed my knuckles. "See you in the morning, *milaya moya*."

I didn't know what he'd said but his eyes had held tenderness and his usually deep voice a little lighter.

"Yes. You will."

Chapter Thirteen

I slept soundly. My body taking the sleep it had craved for several days.

Wearing the short black nightdress, I padded across the room the next morning and opened the curtains.

"Wow."

Stretching out before me was a huge expanse of virgin snow and in the distance trees crowned long, low hills. We'd seen plenty of snow yesterday but lots of it had been over industrial areas and with a gray sky. This, however, was a clear, blue day and the sight was truly spectacular.

There was a quiet knock at the door. "Samantha?"

"Yes, come in." I slipped back onto the bed.

Darya peeked around the door holding a cup of coffee, the scent of which quickly reached my highly sensitive-to-caffeine nose.

"How did you sleep?" she asked, walking over and passing me the drink.

"Thanks." I took a sip. "Really well. The bed is so comfortable and I was exhausted. Sorry if I wasn't much company at dinner last night."

She smiled. "You were great, do not worry. And I am glad the bed was comfortable."

"More importantly," I said. "How is your father this morning?"

"The van came with the oxygen a couple of hours ago. It is a big..." She made a tall, long shape with her hands.

"A cylinder?"

"Yes, I think so, a cylinder. And he has had it on his nose for a while. It has made a big difference already."

"That's great news. And if he can have oxygen here rather than hospital that's better for him. Everyone likes to be in their own home when they're sick."

"Yes, he wouldn't eat or sleep in hospital. He would just be sad and lonely without my mother. Forty-five years married and they won't be in separate beds." She smiled. "Vadmir is waiting for you."

"Really? Why?"

"He says he is taking you for a walk, to the forest."

"What now? This early?"

Darya laughed. "It is not early, it is nearly lunchtime."

I groaned. "Oh, I'm so sorry. I guess I'll never get used to switching time zones."

"It is okay, no problem."

"Can you tell Vadmir I'll just shower and then I'll be ready."

"Of course, and would you like bread and sausage before you go?"

"No, no, thanks. Perhaps just some fruit."

"Yes, we have berries, is that okay?"

"Perfect."

An hour later and Vadmir and I were crawling along a snow-laden track into the mountains. He'd attached snow-chains to the BMW's wheels and it was coping just fine.

"There are great views from up here, it's worth the trip," he said.

"The views are stunning from the apartment. I had no idea when we arrived last night what was around me."

He grinned. "Yes, they are very good."

"I'm pleased your father is feeling better today."

"He looks better. The nurse who came this morning thinks he'll be up soon, now that he is on the right medication."

"That will be great."

"I've promised to watch the game with him later. Vipers, Bruins, is that okay with you?"

I reached over and pressed my hand on his arm, over his jacket. "You don't need to ask me, you're here to spend time with him. I'm just hanging on for the ride and enjoying meeting your family."

"They're enjoying meeting you."

"I hope so."

"Oh, look, we are here," he said.

A small clearing with a snow-covered bench and trashcan lay just ahead.

"This was one of my favorite places to bring my girlfriend, Alena, when I was a teenager," he said. "It was a long bike ride but on a sunny day it was worth the trip. You rarely see anything here except moose and the odd black bear."

"Bear?"

He laughed. "Do not worry, I will protect you."

"I'm not so sure." The thought of a bear attack didn't appeal. I'd seen those documentaries where people out on strolls or camping trips were mauled and their innards spilt over the woodland floor.

"Hey, don't look so scared. We won't see bears today, they're... what do you call it...asleep, for the winter."

"Hibernating."

"Yes, hibernating."

"That's a relief."

"But even in the summer, they're more scared of us than we are of them. They run a mile when they smell a human. They're not like those big grizzlies you get in Canada. Now those *I* would run from."

"Me, too."

He pulled the car to a halt, the front facing a gap in the trees that allowed a long, uninterrupted view into the valley.

"It's beautiful," I said, unbuckling and leaning forward.

"It sure is." He pulled the keys from the ignition. "You want to walk?"

"Yes, definitely."

"Wait there."

As usual he rounded the car and opened my door for me. I placed my gloved hand in his and he squeezed it and didn't let go as he shut the car and clicked the fob to lock it.

"We'll go this way," he said, tugging me to the right. "But not too far, it is really cold today."

The air was already nipping my cheeks and I was glad of the warm layers I had on.

As we walked down a winding track our boots squeaked in the deep snow. The forest was perfectly still and absolutely silent. Not a breath of wind, no sign of life.

"Footprints," Vadmir said, suddenly pointing downward.

I looked at the enormous dents in the snow. There were signs of life. "What are they from?"

"Moose."

"Wow, big feet."

"Yes, they are big. Luckily they don't herd."

"Don't they?"

"No, they live alone, and they're usually...er...grumpy."

"I didn't know that. Are they dangerous?"

"No, not if you avoid them and don't go out of your way to anger them."

"Hey, look," I said, pointing at a flash of red running up a tree. "A red squirrel."

"They wake up sometimes for food in the winter, cute to see." He released my hand and put his arm around my shoulder. "Are you warm enough?"

"Yes, thanks to my new coat and hat."

"And the boots? Your feet are warm, yes?"

"Yes, very." I reached up and placed a kiss on his cheek. He hadn't shaved and his bristles were soft on my lips. "Thank you."

He smiled and hugged me closer. It felt so natural to be like this with him, natural and comfortable.

We carried on walking. The sharp fresh air and the peace was good for my soul after hours of working at thirty-five thousand feet, and I enjoyed the space around me.

"Watch this," Vadmir said, stopping and reaching for a low bough.

He gave it a good shake and the whole pine tree seemed to shiver under his energetic yanking.

A flurry of snow spilled down, covering him and me.

"Hey," I laughed, brushing it from my shoulders.

He took no notice and shook harder, reached for another branch and tumbled a big lump down that skimmed the tip of my nose and covered the front of my coat.

"Watch it," I said, laughing again.

"Or else what?" he said. His cheeks were reddening and plumes of hot air puffed from his mouth.

"Or this." I quickly stooped, gathered a bunch of snow in my hands, formed a ball and threw it at him.

Surprise flashed over his eyes when it hit him right in the center of his chest. The white splattered outwards on his dark coat and the noise of the hit a sudden *whump* echoing into the forest.

"Right," he said, pursing his lips and bending over. "You've started a war now."

His hastily made snowball was suddenly hurtling toward me. It collided with my right shoulder, breaking up instantly.

Again I stooped, created my next weapon and hurled it back.

He was gathering another lump of snow and as he looked up the one I'd just thrown hit him on his forehead, over his hat, covering his face in snow.

I yelped. "Whoops!"

"You're too good," he said, throwing his ball at me but missing. "So I'm not going to take it easy on you anymore just because you're a girl."

Another snowball was already whizzing toward me. I dodged to the left, made a half-hearted attempt at returning another one and then turned and ran.

He got me in the back, the snowy missile colliding with a soft *thump*. "Vadmir," I shrieked, suppressing a giggle. "No." I increased my speed, the cold air rushing into my lungs.

"Come back," he shouted as another ball skimmed past my ear.

I picked up the pace, but it was no good. I could hear him behind me, his footsteps hard and fast. His breaths loud.

Big arms wrapped around my waist and suddenly I was flying through the air, held tight against him.

We landed with me on top in a huge drift of snow.

He was grinning, snow flakes covered his hat and sat in his eyelashes.

"You big bully," I said, slipping my gloved hands up his jacket to rest at his collar.

"You started it," he said.

"Only because you covered me in snow from the tree."

He licked his lips. "So let's call it quits and make up with a kiss."

I pretended to think about it, rolling my eyes upward and twisting my mouth.

"Go on, you know you want to."

He was right. I did. Ever since that sweet kiss the night before I'd wanted to kiss him again. Feel him against me, like this, sample his flavor and become the focus of his attention.

"I guess," I said.

He cupped my face, the palms of his gloves cold, and tugged me closer. Our lips touched, a spot of warmth on otherwise cool skin.

"Sammy."

"Yes?"

"I really like kissing you. I like doing lots of things with you, but kissing." He brushed his mouth over mine again. "That I really like."

I smiled and he captured me again, this time for a more intense kiss. Some of the heated passion I knew he kept inside seeped out. There was a hint of urgency to him now and taste of desire.

He held me tighter even though our clothing was bulky. The hardness of his body, lying beneath mine pressed into me—chest, belly, thighs.

I had a sudden desperate wish to be back in the privacy of a warm hotel room. Somewhere we could give in to our carnal desires. Let our lust run free and get naked and sweaty.

"We should go back to the car," he said, shifting. "Before you get cold."

"I'm okay."

He smiled. "Even so, you are not used to these sub-zero temperatures."

He stood as though I hadn't been sprawled on top of him, hoisting me up at the same time as he got to his feet. He took an awkward step forward and grimaced.

"Are you okay?" I asked, suddenly worried that he'd twisted something in the fall. Damn, what if he'd injured himself and wouldn't be able to play? We shouldn't have messed around like that.

"Yeah." He straightened to his full height and pulled in a breath.

"Vadmir? You're not. Have you hurt yourself?"

He huffed. "No, it is just...having you on top of me has created a problem in my pants."

"Oh..." I smiled. "Sorry."

He shrugged and smiled. "You can't help being a sexy minx."

"Let's go back to the car," I said, winding my arm around the snowy waist of his jacket. "If you can make it that far."

"You are cheeky, too," he said, looping his arm around my shoulder.

Before we got back in the car we brushed off our coats and hats and put them, along with our gloves, in the rear seats.

Vadmir turned the heater up and found a classic radio station. He set it to a low background noise. It wasn't a piece I recognized.

He rubbed his hands together and turned to me. His nose was a little pink and his eyes all the bluer in the sheer whiteness of our surroundings. "Shall we go?"

"But what about the problem in your pants?" I asked. I'd had a wicked thought and with it came a flutter of excitement in my belly.

"It's still there." He shifted on the seat.

"Do you want me to help you out with that before we head back?"

He tipped his eyebrows. "What?"

"The problem?" I directed my gaze at his groin. "Do you need helping out?"

He'd been right, there was an uncomfortable issue going on there, and it seemed to be getting worse by the second. I could make out the long thick line of his cock pressing against his pants. The zipper looked fit to burst.

"I'd be damn grateful if you would." He kept his face deadly serious but there was a sexy, naughty glint in his eye that made my pussy tremble.

I pushed my hair behind my ears and sidled closer to him. "How about if we do this?" I found the top button on his pants and released it. "Does that help?"

"Not really," he said, placing one hand on the door as if he were relaxing as he drove along on a sunny day.

"How about this?" I searched for his zipper and then slowly drew it down.

He groaned as the release eased over his shaft.

"That must be better," I said, brushing my lips over his chin and then kissing to the angle of his jawline.

"Yes." He continued to sit very still, as though enjoying the fact I was taking the lead, teasing him.

"I can feel the root of this problem now," I said, cupping him through the material. "It's quite a big one."

"Sammy," he said, breathily. "Fuck."

"No, we're not going to fuck here, it's too cold to get naked."

He swallowed. "So don't get me going."

"Oh, I'm not going to leave you with a problem." I met my lips with his. "Don't worry about that."

I stroked along his length, found the tip and squeezed. "How about we slip these pants down a bit?"

He didn't need asking twice. A quick shift and his pants were at his thighs and his cock free and proud, jutting upward.

I wrapped my hand around the shaft, set up a slow push-pull motion and licked my lips. "You keep watch for anyone," I said. "While I get to work."

He opened his mouth, as if about to say something but then shut it again. His eyes were a little glazed. He was breathing heavily.

I dipped downward, glad of the space the large car had given us. The tip of his cock was a dark mauve color, at odds with the pallor of the rest of his skin. The slit was deep and wide and as I rubbed his shaft from base to tip again a tiny sheen of moisture developed.

"Sammy," he said, resting his free hand on my head. "I dreamt of your mouth on me again. Last night. This is what I dreamt of. This."

A thrill went through me at his confession. "Was it a good dream?"

"Hell yeah."

"Did I do this?" I opened up and took him on a fast, deep ride to the back of my throat.

His hips bucked. "Ahh...*dah,dah*. Yes, yes. Just like that. Fuck."

I sucked up, using my fingers to massage his erection as it was exposed.

His fingers tightened in my hair.

Allowing him to drop completely from my mouth, I lifted my head a little. "There isn't anyone around, is there?"

"No, damn it. No, don't worry about that, not here. It's deserted. Don't stop."

I smiled. I'd just wanted to hear the desperation in his voice. I knew there wouldn't be anyone out there. "I'll carry on then, shall I?"

"Yes... I think you should."

I set to work. Industriously maneuvering him in and out of my mouth. My hands and my tongue were both busy. He tasted how he smelled. Manly and woody and the scent reminded me of all the screaming orgasms we'd shared on our two wild nights together. I'd taken him in my mouth on the second night, but he'd been in control, now it was me calling the shots.

My heart raced and my panties dampened. Damn, if we'd been in a bed now I'd turn around and get my pussy over his face so he could lick me at the same time as I fellated him. That would sort me out perfectly.

I trembled as a delicious shiver ran up my spine at the erotic image.

"Oh, yeah..." he gasped. "It's too good."

I didn't let up. Salty pre-cum was basting my tongue and I wanted more. I wanted his seed, his pleasure.

He pushed my head down onto his cock. Not hard but enough for me to know his restraint was reaching the limit.

Increasing the speed of my hand jerking the base of his erection, I laved at his glans.

He tensed beneath me and barked out several sharp Russian words.

I was breathing fast, so was he. His cock was so hard in my hands and in my mouth. My jaw ached, as did my wrist, but I didn't let up.

Then it was there, the first spurt of his release.

"*Yebat', vot eto*," he cried out, hunching over me and trapping me in his groin.

A second wave of pleasure burst from him.

I drank him up. The thickness of his semen sliding down my throat in waves.

"Please," he said, "that's it. Oh... Sammy..."

It wasn't and I kept on sucking him as his final jet of cum flooded my mouth.

Only when I was sure he was spent and his cock had lost its rigidity did I raise my head.

I rubbed my tongue around my lips. They were swollen and hot. "Has that sorted out the problem?"

"I think we...can say yes...it has." He blew out a breath, adding to the mist that had fogged the windows, then he kissed me, hard.

Chapter Fourteen

We stopped at a grocery store on the way back to the apartment and Vadmir stocked up on supplies for watching the game with his father. Cheesy nachos were a must, apparently, and an acquired taste Ruslan had developed since Vadmir had introduced them to him several years ago.

"You want to watch it with us?" Vadmir asked as we hung our coats in the hallway and kicked off our boots. "It will be a good one."

"No, you have time with your father."

"You would make his day if you did."

I frowned. "Really?"

"Yeah, he likes you." He touched his lips to my temple and pulled me close. "But not as much as I do."

It made me feel warm inside when Vadmir let his voice go all low and husky and he said such nice things. It was something I could get used to. "Well, okay then. But you're going to have to explain the rules. I'm not exactly a hockey expert."

"Ah, it's easy, nothing to it. Puck either goes in the net or it doesn't."

"I'm sure there's more to it than that."

He grinned and released me. "A little bit."

We set up trays of food and went into the bedroom. Ruslan was sitting up, a small plastic tube beneath his nose and a black oxygen tank at his side. He was a much brighter color than the day before. His lips had lost the blue tinge and his cheeks glowed pink instead of sallow gray. There was a definite healthier vibe about him, as though he'd had an injection of energy.

"Samantha," he said, smiling.

I grinned back. "You look much better," I said.

Vadmir translated.

"He feels much better," Vadmir said, "and he's just informed me that your beautiful presence has made this a perfect day."

I laughed and touched Ruslan's shoulder. "You old charmer."

Again Vadmir translated and Ruslan nodded and laughed.

I suspected it was having his son at his side that had improved Ruslan's mood so much, not my being here. But it was wonderful to see him looking so much better than when we'd arrived. The treatment the doctor had prescribed and Vadmir's idea to bring the hospital to him was clearly doing the trick.

Vadmir pulled us both a chair up, beside the bed. He then scrolled through the television channels until he found the pre-recorded game he and his father wanted to watch.

I joined the two men in a bottle of beer and nibbled at the nachos.

The game started loud and fast. Horns, cheers and shouts from the crowd as the teams skated onto the ice with a great blast of *Sex on Fire*.

Vadmir spoke to his father and then to me. "Speed is in goal but I expect Jackson will get a chance."

"Jackson, isn't he the guy—?"

"Your friend hooked up with, yeah."

"I wonder if he's recovered."

"From her?"

"Well, yes, but she's been ill from the shrimp they had. I'd imagine he got it, too."

Vadmir pulled a face. "I haven't heard but then I've been pretty out of touch these last few days." He leaned close. "And distracted."

I breathed deep, his body scent was laced with sex, to my nose at least, and heat from his skin drifted onto my cheeks.

He grinned and returned his attention to the game, slugged on his beer.

The on-screen music changed, a chant like song in English. I guessed it was lyrics from some heavy metal band.

"Ladies and gentlemen, boys and girls, please bring your attention to me. A spectacle for your eyes to see. A whirlwind of catastrophe. Like nothing you've witnessed before. Watch closely as I open this door. Your jaws will be on the floor. After this you'll be begging for more, more, more..."

The players circled each other and took their starting positions. The Vipers in blood-red and the Bruins in black and gold.

"That's the captain, isn't it?" I said, spotting a Viper player with Lewis written on the back of his jersey.

"Hey, you do know something."

I shrugged. "He walked out with another player, just before you did that day."

"Lucky he's got a hot lady for himself otherwise he'd have snapped you up quicker than you can say puck."

"Don't be daft."

"I am not." He winked, turned to his father and began to chat in Russian.

I didn't mind not understanding what was being said. I was happy to watch the hockey. The camera was panning around the audience. There was a medley of adults, kids, male and female. Banners were being waved including a large one held flattened on the Plexi by a pretty girl with long dark hair that said, *"I love you Brick. I'm 18 now. Call me!"*

I remembered Brick's swagger as he'd strolled past Harmony and me. There was no doubt about it, he had a certain something and a damn cute ass. No wonder he had an army of girls wishing their teenage years away so they could dream of catching him.

The game started and I sat forward in the chair, munched on another nacho.

The puck whizzed around so fast it was hard to see where it was. Within seconds the Bruins scored—a fast slap shot down the wing and then a neat wrist flick into the goal.

"Ah, *chto eto pustaya trata,*" Vadmir said, tutting and then shaking his head.

Ruslan blew out a breath and looked distressed.

"Your goaltender missed that one by miles," I said.

"He doesn't usually. Speed is the best in the business," Vadmir said. "I wonder where his head is?"

The teams faced off. The puck flying neatly into Viper possession. I made an effort to read the names on the backs of the jerseys so I could keep up. Lewis had the puck, he tapped it to Starr who sneaked it through the legs of a Bruin to Taylor.

"Go, go, go." Vadmir stood, giving me a great view of his cute ass. "Do it, Phoenix."

I craned my neck to see around Vadmir.

Phoenix was tapping the puck left to right and heading straight for the goal. He'd left all of the Bruin defense behind. I didn't think he was ever going to fire, he got so close to the goaltender but then he did, one neat, short slide and the back of the net was whacked outward by the puck.

"Yes." Vadmir punched the air. "That's more like it. Go Vipers. Get it on."

The opposition goaltender lay on the floor, his skates banging the ice like a child having a tantrum.

The Vipers piled against the boards, jumping on the scorer, slapping his back and high-fiving each other.

"What a goal by Phoenix. Talk about talent," the commentator shouted. "Time and time again he delivers. You have to see it to believe it."

Ruslan chattered in Russian. I didn't know what he was saying but his excitement was infectious and I grinned and nodded, sharing my attention between the screen and him.

Vadmir replied to his father then sat back down. He leaned across and tapped my knee. "Good, yes?"

"Yes, very good."

The game started up again. I could feel the excitement rolling off the two men in the room.

The Vipers struggled to gain the puck. The Bruins were now running rings around them. Brick crashed into one and sent him sprawling, without any apparent attempt at getting the puck but the ref did nothing.

The home crowd erupted. Clearly irritated by Brick's action.

But the Bruins still had control. Playing with the Vipers—tormenting and teasing and getting ever closer to scoring another point.

"Come on," Vadmir said. "Get to it, Raven. Support Reed." He turned to Ruslan and spoke again.

Ruslan replied then leaned forward, teeth gritted. "*Vne igry!*"

"*Dah*, off side." Vadmir slugged the last of his beer then banged the bottle on the table.

I wondered if he felt guilty about not playing with his team. For being halfway around the world when they needed him there, doing his stuff.

Suddenly a ruck broke out. Two players battling for the puck had hit the boards at the same time, the puck was then stolen and sent to the opposite end of the arena.

"And Kenzie has taken offense to that," the commentator shouted. "Here we go."

I saw that it was Brick who'd got himself tangled in the fight. The sticks were down and they were squaring up.

"Ah, fuck," Vadmir said, "not again."

"What? What again?"

"Brick, he can't stay out of trouble."

In a tangle of arms and legs Kenzie and Brick dragged at each other and tried to land punches. It was almost comical watching them fight on the ice. Their legs were slipping in all directions as they struggled to keep their balance.

The crowd was going wild. As if this was their favorite part of the game.

Two linesmen in black and white striped tops joined the fracas, trying to separate the players and narrowly missing being hit themselves.

Brick was down on his knees. He took a couple of hits to the head.

"*Vstavat*," Ruslan shouted.

"Get up," Vadmir yelled.

I held my breath and wondered how they were allowed to get away with this violence.

Brick found his feet again, socked his opponent in the guts and then got one around his head in return.

Ruslan started jabbering. I had no idea what he was saying but I knew he wouldn't have been able to talk that fast when we'd first arrived. So if nothing else that was a good sign.

"And Kenzie is trying to get another right hook in," the commentator jabbered. "And here we go, Phoenix is in on the action!"

He was right, but it wasn't just Phoenix, it was two other Bruin players and Raven and Lewis. Another linesman jumped in but was floored immediately.

Still the crowd went wild. Clapping, cheering, banging on the Plexi.

"I had no idea they fought like this," I said. "Do you do that?" I pointed at the screen and looked at Vadmir.

His attention was on the action. "What?"

"Do you fight like that?"

"Er, no...never."

Somehow I didn't think that was quite the truth. They were all at it. There was barely one member of either team not pulling, pushing, shoving or aiming a punch at another player.

"Shall I get some more beer?" I asked, standing and picking up Vadmir's empty bottle.

"Yeah, great."

I left the room, leaving the on-screen chaos behind.

"Hey, Samantha, how is it in there?" Dayra called from the living area.

"Okay, your father seems much better." I peered in. She was sitting with her feet up watching TV. Fresh home from work she still wore a green shop apron.

"Yes, he is better today. Is he enjoying the game?" she asked.

"I think so, though there seems to be as much fighting as playing hockey."

"Ah, it is always like that. I think that is one of the reasons they enjoy it. You should see some of the bruises Vadmir used to come home with. He split his eye and his lip more times than I could count. Always fighting, always landing in the out-of-time box."

"Ah, okay." I nodded. It was just as I'd thought, Vadmir was no stranger to fighting or time-out. "Catch you later."

I grabbed some more of the beers Vadmir and I had picked up earlier and wandered back into the bedroom.

The fight had ended and play had resumed.

"Brick and Kenzie are on the bench," Vadmir said. "Four minutes."

"Is that bad?"

"Yeah, we need Brick. But we are used to him coming on and off the ice. It's a habit of his, fighting."

I remembered seeing Brick with his cute smile and golden curls. Clearly he wasn't as angelic as his image projected. Much the same as Vadmir wasn't quite the pacifist he would have me believe he was.

"Here you go." I set down more beer.

Ruslan smiled his thanks but waved his beer away.

"One is enough for him these days," Vadmir said. "And probably sensible with his medication."

"I agree." I sat next to Vadmir again and he touched the base of his bottle with mine, winked and then turned back to the screen.

He was clearly enjoying himself and as the puck dodged around the rink, a few near hits for both teams, he and his father chattered enthusiastically, creating their own commentary over and above what was on the television.

I relaxed back and watched the game. I didn't understand the complexities but as Vadmir had said, you just have to get the puck in the net.

It was clear the Vipers were a great team and I could see why Vadmir adored them so much. It was also obvious they were struggling to keep the scoreboard even. The Bruins were great at their job.

The game came to an end. With even scores after overtime I couldn't see who would be declared winner.

"What happens now?" I asked.

"Penalty shoot out," Vadmir said.

"Are the Vipers good at that?"

"The best."

"And here is our must-watch player," the commentator shouted. "Let's hope Phoenix gets the Vipers off to a good start. He's on fire at the moment. Totally unstoppable."

The Bruin goaltender ducked from left to right. The camera panned back and I could see the Viper player, Phoenix, racing toward the puck that sat waiting in the center circle.

Excitement churned within me. I wanted the Vipers to score, get that point.

"And here we go, he's got it, he's going, he's... it's innnnnn."

"Yes," Vadmir shouted, punching the air. "Great start."

Ruslan clapped enthusiastically and grinned.

"And now for Bruins' hot-shot Kenzie, he's got something to prove," the commentator said. "He missed last week's crucial point so will that give him the guts he needs to pull this one out of the bag?"

I knotted my fingers and watched as the Viper goaltender hovered with his knees just about on the ice, he was jerking this way and that, trying to guess the way the Bruin player would shoot.

"Yes, it's another point!" the commentator shouted as Kenzie scored.

"Fuck," Vadmir said, banging his beer on the table.

"Now who is it?" I asked.

"Raven, he's a defenseman but great at these shots."

"Okay."

A big, dark player circled the opposite end of the rink. His teammates half hung over the boards shouting and thumping the air. The excitement was tangible.

"And here he goes, it's always a treat to watch," the commentator yelled. "And he's scored."

"Yes," I yelled.

Ruslan yelped in delight and then coughed.

Vadmir patted his father on the back.

"And Starr has got another trick to add to his repertoire," the commentator shouted, "he's lightning fast. Lefebre didn't even see that heading his way. Who the hell would want Raven Starr coming at them in a shootout? Not me, that's for sure."

Vadmir poured his father some water and then, once satisfied he was okay, sat back down.

The next Bruin player took to the rink. He whizzed around, his jersey flattening against his body with the speed he was going. He appeared to try and copy Raven, one fast dash to the goal and a wrist flick.

"And he's missed, it's headed back to center rink. He's going to be bummed about that," the commentator said.

"Serves him right, cocky ass," Vadmir muttered.

"Who is that?" I asked, sensing history.

"Bailey, he's a dirty player."

"Really?"

"Yeah."

"Why, what's happened?"

Vadmir looked at me. "I had to take his skates out and teach him a lesson last season."

"You mean you got in a fight?" I raised my eyebrows, wondering if he'd admit it.

He frowned. "Yeah, I guess."

"Did you win?"

"What do you think?"

"I don't know, that's why I asked."

"Of course I won." He huffed as if the possibility of not winning a fight was ludicrous.

"Oh...good."

He shrugged. "I got concussion and ended up in ER but he was worse."

I studied his face and wondered not just how his nose had stayed so neat and straight with all this fighting but also how I'd managed to get myself involved with such a fist-happy caveman. I sighed, oh, well, he had other attributes and as long as the fists were only free and easy on the ice I could live with it.

Ruslan spoke excitedly and pointed at the screen.

"Here we go," Vadmir said. "Lewis is taking the last shot. If he gets this the game is ours."

I leaned forward, crossed my fingers and held my breath.

Lewis was racing up to the puck. Two refs were shadowing him. The Bruin goaltender was dangerously far from his goal.

"Ohhh..." I said, knowing it would all happen super-fast.

Lewis knocked the puck from left to right.

"And Lewis is holding it, holding it..." the commentary gabbled. "holding it, and he's turned and oh, my goodness, through the legs. I have never seen anything like it and the Vipers have won."

Vadmir leaped into the air, his feet coming off the ground and then shaking the oxygen tank when he landed on the floor with a thump. "*Dah*! Fuck yes!"

Ruslan clapped enthusiastically and grinned. He didn't take his eyes off Vadmir, clearly enjoying his son's celebration and having him at his side.

Vadmir turned, planted a kiss on his father's head and then swung 'round to me and smacked my lips with a big kiss, too.

"Thank God," he said. "They needed those points."

"It's great." I grinned.

"Yes." He pulled in a deep breath and when he let it out it was as if a weight had left him. "It is. It is all great."

Chapter Fifteen

"Are you ready?" Vadmir asked me after breakfast the next morning.

"Yes, just my hair to do."

He studied my head and looked bemused. "What is there to do with it?"

"I haven't finished curling it."

"Haven't you?"

"No."

I could tell by his expression that the concept of curling hair was lost on him.

"I won't be long, twenty minutes or so."

He glanced at his watch. "Really?"

"Yes, it takes a bit longer than yours."

He scrubbed his hand over his crew cut. "I guess."

I grabbed my coffee from the table. "I'll be quick."

"Yep."

We were going to the local rink where he'd learned to skate. Apparently he always called in when home; saw his old coaches, friends and the new talent coming up the ranks. For a small place, so he'd told me, Sokol was blessed with great players.

Deciding not to overly fuss with my hair, we were soon heading across the river toward the rink on the west side of town.

"You smell nice," he said, turning down the heater now that the car was warm.

"Thanks."

He glanced at me. "Like flowers."

"It's Clarins, you bought it for me."

He raised his eyebrows. "I did?"

"Yes, the receptionist at the hotel brought me a bag of Clarins toiletries, this was in it."

"I like that I bought it for you, even if I didn't know." He shook his head. "You really hadn't intended on staying that night when you came from the airport, had you?"

"I don't know what I thought." I shrugged. "I guess just a few hours with you or something."

"Just enough time to fuck each other stupid."

"Yes, except we fucked each other unconscious and I missed my flight." I gestured out of the window. It was beginning to snow again. "I should be in Miami now, lying by a pool with a mojito."

"Sorry."

"It's okay."

"I'll take you," he said, resting his hand on my knee.

"Where?"

"Miami, when we get back to Orlando. We'll go for a weekend, you can drink as many mojitos as you want and lounge by the pool to your head's content."

"My what?" I smiled. He'd done it again.

"Content, 'til your head is content."

I laughed. "You mean heart's content."

He frowned and replaced his hand on the steering wheel. "If you say so."

I leaned across and kissed his cheek. "That sounds wonderful. I'd love to go to Miami with you."

"You would?" He sounded surprised and turned to me again.

"Yeah, I bet you look great in swim trunks."

He grinned. "And I bet you look amazing in a bikini. In fact, we might not get out of the hotel room come to think of it."

"Yes, that does seem to be a problem we have."

Sokol ice rink appeared run down and small after seeing the Vipers' magnificent home in Orlando the week before. It had clearly had very little money spent on it for decades, but the enthusiasm and smiles of the people inside made up for that.

"Vadmir," an excited voice called as we wandered in.

"Ivan," Vadmir said, striding up to a middle-aged guy with a short goatee beard.

I stepped to one side and watched as they did the usual three kisses and then began to chatter in Russian. I realized just how much I loved hearing Vadmir speak in his natural language. It was sexy and husky and suited him so well. I probably shouldn't be so harsh on him for getting a few English words mixed up when I could barely remember one word of his language.

"Sammy," Vadmir said, holding his hand out to me. "Meet Ivan, he was my coach through my teenage years."

"Ivan," I said, with a smile and moving out of the shadows of the wall.

Ivan greeted me enthusiastically with much cheek kissing and approving looks to Vadmir. He gestured to his hair and I guessed he was commenting on mine.

Vadmir placed his forearm over my shoulder and pulled me against his side. He looked down at me. "I'm going to put skates on and give the guys a training session. You okay to hang out here?"

"Yes, of course."

"You can grab a coffee from the machine."

"I'm fine. I've had plenty."

"Sure."

"Yeah, so go show me what you can do, Russian boy."

"I think you already know what I can do." He dropped a quick kiss to my lips and then strode off. "And I know you like it," he threw over his shoulder.

I found a seat at the end of a long row of blue plastic benches and tucked myself out of the way. It gave me a good vantage point and I could see the coffee machine if I decided I needed caffeine and heat.

There were already several players on the ice, knocking pucks around and weaving in and out of cones. A couple of guys in opposite goals were padded up and doing their best to stop shots.

I made the most of the alone time and called Harmony and then Patrick. Harmony was on the mend and Patrick, like Nicola had been, was perfectly nice about my oversleeping but I sensed an underlying note of disappointment. But that disaster felt a million miles away, up here in the Arctic Circle. And even missing my holiday in Miami didn't feel so bad now that Vadmir had said we'd go together. That thought appealed to me very much. I wondered if we'd go this month.

After ten minutes Vadmir shot onto the ice with Ivan at his side. He was tall anyway, but the additional inches his skates gave him meant he looked enormous. His must have had padding on beneath his black jersey, too, because his already wide shoulders were now colossal.

There was a chorus of whoops and cheers from the young guys on the ice and many of them tapped sticks with Vadmir who was grinning broadly beneath his cage helmet.

Ivan eventually calmed everyone down and Vadmir took over the training.

I folded my arms to keep the warmth close to my body, and watched him patiently helping line shots up, advising the forward and the keeper and then setting exercises.

The rink was filled with the sounds of blades on ice, pucks sliding and hitting the boards and deep Russian voices. Several other spectators gathered, men and women and a few young kids. I guessed word had got out that an All-Star player was in town.

Eventually the hour came to an end, all the players slid to the opposite side of the rink and then stomped onto the hard floor leaving the ice eerily empty.

When Vadmir disappeared out of view I went for coffee. My toes were cold as were my hands, even in gloves. The vending machine was onerous, taking more of my kopecks than it should. But eventually I had a paper cup with something warm and brown in it that smelled vaguely like coffee.

Leaving my gloves off, I cupped it in my palms and walked back to where I'd been sitting.

The few spectators had drifted off and I sat, planning on waiting for Vadmir to come find me when he was finished.

The coffee was weak and contained sugar, which I didn't normally take. I sipped it and held the cup until it was cool and then went on the hunt for a trashcan. I'd expected Vadmir to have returned by now.

I spotted a blue plastic bin with a black liner wrinkled around the top and headed for it. I dropped the cup inside and then wandered deeper into the back corridors of the rink.

Voices filtered toward me, from around the next corner. One was deep, it sounded like Vadmir.

I continued walking, the soles of my new boots utterly silent, as I eased my gloves back on.

Just before I rounded the corner I paused. It was gloomy here and the voices echoed. It was a little creepy. But also now I was sure one was Vadmir's and the other, that was female.

Hesitating for just a second, I then stepped into view.

I'd been right, it was Vadmir, and he was talking to a woman. She wore a caramel colored coat that I'd bet was real fur. Cascading from a hat that matched her coat, she had straight dark hair, nearly as long as mine. Even from here I could see she was stunningly beautiful with large doe-like eyes and scarlet lips, skin as smooth as china.

I stopped and shifted into the shadows, not hiding but not announcing my presence, either. My attention had been caught because they were talking in urgent tones plus Vadmir's hand gestures were agitated.

She turned from him, faced away and bowed her head.

He rested his hand on her shoulder, moved in close behind and spoke into her ear.

A swell of nausea rolled through me. What I was witnessing was an intimate gesture, one that suggested they were more than passing acquaintances—more than friends.

He was talking again, in hushed tones, the sound mumbling toward me through the cool, shadowed corridor. I had no idea what he was saying but he rubbed her shoulders as he did so. Soothingly, the way I had him the night before when he'd been upset.

Suddenly she turned again and looked up at him.

He dropped his hands. I thought he might step back from her, she looked so angry. But he didn't, instead he raised his chin and stared down at her with his jaw set.

She spoke again, short clipped words.

He shook his head from side to side.

She pursed her lips and glared up at him.

For a moment it seemed they were having a staring competition but then she spun from him and strutted my way.

She wore high-heeled boots that clattered noisily and the sound ricocheted around the corridor like a string of bullets.

I had no time to move or run, so, shoving my hands into my pockets, I pulled in a deep breath. A gut feeling assured me she wasn't about to be my new best buddy. Instinct told me she was a rival.

Her gaze landed on me and she faltered for a second, her tapping heels pausing briefly. Then she strode forward as if with renewed irritation, arms swinging, chin held high.

I bit on my bottom lip and glanced at Vadmir, who was standing with his hands on his hips, his cap pulled low and his feet apart.

She set her gaze on me, not blinking, just staring. No smile, no greeting, only an arctic glare.

"*I vot teper' etot,*" she said, suddenly spinning to face Vadmir. "*Vy privezti yeye syuda.*"

"*Dah,*" he said, "I did bring her here." He looked from her to me. His eyebrows were pulled low and his mouth a tight, straight line.

She huffed, tossed her hair over her shoulder, and after one final withering look my way, marched around the corner.

I stared at the space she'd just occupied. If I'd felt cold before now I was frozen.

"Sammy," Vadmir said, pacing up to me, his long strides making short work of the distance.

"Who was that?" I asked, suppressing a shiver that was trying to prickle its way up my spine.

"Alena."

"You know her." I didn't make it a question, it was a statement. It was obvious they knew each other. "What were you arguing about?"

"You're cold," he said, touching the backs of his fingers to my cheek.

"Yes, but what was going on between you?" I had no right to be jealous. We didn't exactly have a relationship, but I couldn't help it. We were together, for this week at least. Hell I'd sucked him off yesterday, up at the forest. I was staying in his home. "Who is she to you?"

"Just a girl," he said, frowning and dropping his hands to his sides.

"Just a girl," I repeated. The forest. A sudden memory of the forest, something he'd said about taking his girlfriend up there, on bikes, came back to me. Alena? "Girlfriend, you mean?"

"Ex-girlfriend. Come on, let's get out of here. I have done my duty for the rink and the guys." He placed his hand on the small of my back and steered me in the direction I'd just come.

"The girlfriend you used to take to the forest? You said her name was Alena, didn't you?"

He huffed. "You are too clever, Sammy, but yes, Alena is the girl I used to cycle to the forest with, when we were teenagers."

"Which was years ago." A twisting feeling attacked my belly. "So you must be ancient history then. You and her." I knew that wasn't true, not going by the vibes I'd just felt. There was something very present happening, on her part at least. "That was a long time ago, when you were teenagers."

"Yes, it was. A very long time ago."

"So why did she give me a death stare?"

"I am sorry for that."

"Vadmir." I stopped and pressed my hand on his arm. His jacket was thick and puffy. "I know what we've got is a whirlwind of... I don't know, sex, hanging out, whatever. And we don't exactly have any claim on each other, but..." I sighed. "Honesty is good between friends, and we are at least friends." I paused. "Friends with benefits, perhaps, but friends, yes?"

"Yes, friends." He smiled, one side of his mouth tilting and the skin at the corners of his eyes creasing. I loved that smile of his. It was so genuine and warming and made me feel better. "And I agree, honesty is the best programme."

"So," I said, "Who is she and why is she so angry that you brought me here?"

"She was my first love and I hers, but as you said it was a long time ago. A decade ago, longer, from when we first started dating."

I swallowed and beat down an image of them together at the forest, naked, her doing the things I liked doing with Vadmir. I thought of him as a younger man, learning the ropes of sex. Exploring the female form for the first time and discovering all of those deliciously dirty things he knew now that made my body sing.

"So what went wrong?" I asked.

"I went to America."

I hadn't been expecting that. "But you said you'd only been there four years."

"Yes, that's right."

"And you were still together before you went, from being teenagers?"

He nodded. "We were, yes."

"But surely you were serious by then. After all of that time."

"We were, well at least I was, but she wouldn't come with me." He shrugged and the rustling of his jacket material was noisy in the silent arena. "She wouldn't wait for me and she wouldn't come to America, either. What choice did I have but to end it? I couldn't sacrifice my career for her, my career is for more than just me, it is for my family, too. We needed money." He sighed. "Dad's health was already bad, even then."

"That must have been a hard choice."

"Not really. I did what I needed to do."

"Well yes, I can understand that."

"Can you?"

"Of course. No one should be made to sacrifice their dreams for another person. You did what you had to do." I slid my hand down his arm and took his hand in mine. "But just for the record, I think she's crazy, she would have loved America."

He smiled suddenly and then touched the tip of his nose to mine. "Maybe, maybe not. I guess I'll never know."

"And is she still in love with you? Is that why she was mad?" I studied his eyes.

"She wouldn't admit it even if she was, but I doubt it. It's just her pride that is hurt. I brought another woman to Sokol, a beautiful American woman." He brushed his lips over mine. "But let's not talk about Alena anymore. We have a wonderful venison broth waiting for us made by Darya."

Chapter Sixteen

The meal Darya had cooked was amazing and I couldn't believe how hungry I was. I wondered if it was the cold that had increased my normally low appetite. But then perhaps it was sitting around a table with Vadmir and his family that had done it. I'd enjoyed passing bowls of food around, sipping wine and admiring the twilight view from the kitchen window—Sokol illuminated by streetlamps with the meandering river weaving through the center was incredibly pretty.

Ruslan had also joined us for the meal, feeling strong enough to move from the bedroom to the dining area. Vadmir had wheeled the heavy cylinder through and Ruslan ate with the small plastic cannula beneath his nose, still delivering the much needed oxygen. He wasn't full of conversation but I guessed that was because of the effort it had taken to move from the bedroom for the first time in weeks.

"So how was Ivan?" Darya asked Vadmir as she scooped up the last of her dinner with a wedge of bread.

"He was good," Vadmir said. "He doesn't change, always wanting more from the team, always pushing."

She tipped her eyebrows. "He did that to you and now look where you are."

"Yes, you are right." He took a slug of his drink.

"And, Samantha, did you enjoy watching or were you cold?" She shuddered. "I always get so cold when watching Vadmir play."

"Yes, it was cold, but I enjoyed it. I've never seen a real live hockey game."

"You haven't?" Vadmir said, turning to me and looking surprised.

"No. I don't get much time off and when I do I prefer warm leisure pursuits."

"Pursuits?" Darya asked frowning.

"Yes, pastimes, things to do."

"Ahh," she said, nodding her understanding of the new word.

Zoya leaned across, touched my arm and held the wine above my empty glass.

"Yes, please." I smiled.

She topped up my drink and studied me as I took a sip and gave her an approving nod. She seemed fascinated by me still, and watched my every move like a hawk. It wasn't unsettling, just a little weird.

"So tell me about these pursuits," Darya said. "What are they?"

"Well, I'm based in Orlando at the moment. I was renting a place with my friend, Harmony, but the lease came up and we decided not to renew because we didn't like the landlord. So I've been using one of the long term rental rooms at the airport, the airline keeps a bunch, until we find somewhere else." I shrugged. "Which will hopefully be soon, I don't like living out of a hotel."

"Somewhere else in Orlando?" she asked.

"Yes, for now, while I do this particular international route. It may well change, that's why I've never bought." I paused, "Well, I haven't bought property but I've bought plenty of other things on my travels." I grinned.

"Oh, tell me," she said.

"Well, clothes, handbags, shoes, makeup, jewelry, you know, nice stuff."

"Designer?"

"Yes, lots of designer. I'm a sucker for a nice label."

"And where do you buy your...stuff from?" she asked.

I smiled and set my knife and fork together in the center of my empty plate. "Paris, Milan, New York, Cape Town, all over the world. Tokyo is great for shopping, too, and last year we were in Sydney for a long weekend."

Her eyes went a little dreamy. "You have such a wonderful life," she said. "All those glamorous places."

"It is fun."

"Hard work, too," Vadmir said, studying me and holding a small glass of vodka near to his lips. "When you are in the air."

I'd already told Darya all about my job and she was equally envious of that. Quizzing me as we'd sat in the living area the evening before.

"I guess so, but I like it."

"Serving passengers?" he said. "You like that?"

"That's part of my job, yes, but the safety of our travelers is my first priority."

"I bet passengers forget that and get cranky," he said.

"Some are crankier than others." I set my gaze on his, tipped my head and suppressed a smile. "And some don't do what they're told when I tell them to."

"Really?" He feigned surprise and also looked as though he was trying not to grin.

"Yes, some go into the galley when they shouldn't, that's out of bounds for passengers."

"And what do they do there, these bad passengers?" he asked.

"Get in the way, harass the crew and..." I swallowed, remembering my shock at him appearing in the galley, grabbing me and then kissing me. It seemed like weeks ago now, not just days.

He knocked back his shot and set the glass down. "What else do they do wrong, Sammy?" He licked his lips. "Tell me?"

"Well, when I eventually get them to return to their seats, they just sit there, silent, brooding, sulking, thinking about..." I let my words trail off. He'd told me he'd sat on the plane thinking about bending me over, fucking me, fucking my ass. That he'd liked my tight skirt and wanted me, wanted me badly, badly enough to consider fucking me in the galley as I looked down at the earth miles below. But I couldn't exactly say that now, not here.

His eyes sparkled. He knew exactly what I wanted to say.

"That's what they do," I said, "the badly behaved passengers. They sit there and watch and think."

He shifted on his seat and pulled in a breath.

I hoped he was remembering what he'd been thinking about and then doing it later that night at the hotel. He'd shoved me against the wall and made me boneless with the strength of my climax. Afterwards he'd carried me to the bed and took what he'd wanted, sliding his cock into my darkest hole and making me come all over again then releasing his pleasure deep inside me.

He ran his finger around the collar of his roll-neck sweater and swallowed.

I smiled, and continued to study his face the way he was studying mine. Oh yeah, he was picturing it all and I'd bet my last ruble that he was as hard as yesterday with every bit as much of a problem going on in his pants.

"Would you like me to help wash up?" I asked Darya as she stood and gathered the empty bowls she'd been stacking.

"No, no, I will do it," she said with a smile.

"Please," I said. "I'd like to help. I could dry."

"Well...okay, thank you. Mother will be helping my father now so I would be glad."

"*Vy mozhete peremeshchat' kislorod seychas,*" Zoya said to Vadmir, standing and brushing breadcrumbs from her ample chest.

"*V odno mgnoveniye.*"

"Why can't you move the oxygen now?" Darya asked, lifting Vadmir's plate from in front of him and throwing a scowl his way. "Mother just said she needs it in the bedroom."

"I will, in a minute." He reached for the vodka and poured another shot with a frown creasing his brow.

I gave him a knowing smile. He couldn't stand because he had an erection, it was plain as day to me, though thankfully not everyone else.

He narrowed his eyes at me and bit on his bottom lip.

A thrill went through me. There was something carnal about his expression, something that made me think if we got a moment alone, I'd pay for making him think about us fucking when we were at the dinner table with his family.

Excitement tickled its way through my body, making my nipples tingle. I'd like to know what he'd do to me, what erotic punishment I'd get.

If only we could have some time alone together. To release some of this tension.

But that didn't look likely to happen. Not with Zoya watching my every move.

* * * *

I slept soundly again, like I had every other night I'd been in the Arefyev home. There was something safe and calm about the apartment, not to mention the bed was warm and comfortable. I might not be catching up on the shopping I'd intended for my week off, but the sleep debt I owed my body was back in credit.

"Sammy," Vadmir said, knocking on my door. "Are you ready now?"

"Almost." It was the third time he'd called for me, but I'd decided to wash my hair that morning and it took an age to dry with Darya's old Babyliss, and I didn't dare go out into the subzero temperature with it damp. My head would freeze.

Vadmir had announced at breakfast that he wanted to go furniture shopping and would I help him pick some pieces out. I was more than happy to; it would make up for the lack of retail therapy.

I plaited my hair in two long bunches that fell over my shoulders. It wasn't a normal style for me but it would work with the furry hat and it was a nice change from the tight up-dos I often wore for flying. My skin was still a little tanned so I applied just a sweep of powder and flick of mascara and a hint of Benefit Ultra Shine in Spiked Punch.

Quickly, I straightened the baby pink sweater I'd opted for that morning and then, after plucking some fluff from my black pants, I wandered out of the bedroom in search of Vadmir.

The apartment was quiet. I noticed Darya's purse missing from the hook she kept it on in the kitchen. She was at work. Ruslan's door was closed and I guessed his nurse was visiting. Zoya was more than likely also in there.

I found Vadmir in the living area, standing by the window with his hands on his hips. He was looking out at the snowy landscape that stretched into the distance.

My gaze was drawn to his ass as I walked over to him. I couldn't help it, there was some kind of magnetic thing going on with me and his cute butt. Today he wore dark, almost black denims and a deep burgundy sweater that stopped just below the waistband of his jeans.

My palms tingled and I had the urge to touch him. It was strange thinking that we'd touched each other so intimately and now we had to keep a distance. Sneak a grope through clothes or snatch a few minutes in the car to satisfy an urge. Not that my urges had been satisfied since we'd arrived in Sokol and I wasn't sure they would be, not when I was due to head back to Moscow tomorrow ready for my early flight the day after.

Before I knew it my hands were on his ass, sliding over the soft rise of his buttocks and exploring the shape of him through the material. Mmm, he felt good.

He stiffened for a second and then turned. "Fuck, I'm glad that's you."

I laughed. "I bet you are."

He grinned and slid his arms around my waist. "Are you okay?"

"Yes, fine." I slipped my hands up his chest and linked them at his nape.

"I like your hair," he said, eyeing up my long plaits.

"Thanks."

He lifted one and rubbed it gently. "Very pretty."

I leaned into him, so that our chests touched.

He dropped his head and pressed a gentle kiss to my lips.

When he pulled back he poked out his tongue. "You taste sugary...delicious."

I smiled and kissed him again. I adored this quiet side to Vadmir. This huge guy who spoke in such an unfathomable language, who'd made hard decisions for the sake of his family and was happy to fly around the world for them on a moments' notice. He was getting to me, there was no doubt about it. Working his way under my skin the same way he'd traveled over it that first night we'd spent together. He was getting into every crease and corner, the very core of me. It was a shame I had to go so soon. That my time here had almost come to an end.

"Vadmir!"

My heart skipped at the sound of Zoya's voice.

He broke the kiss but didn't release me. "*Dah mat'.*"

"*Chto ty delayesh'*,"

"What does it look like I'm doing?" he said, more to me than his mother. "I'm kissing a beautiful woman, the perfect way to start the day."

We drove across the river to the freeway and headed for the larger town of Vologda. Vadmir kept the speed down as the blue skies had gone and in their place heavy snow clouds were dumping their load.

Eventually, after a long crawl in traffic, we reached a large furniture store that was painted blue and had bright yellow writing. As we approached I realized it was IKEA.

"Hey," I said. "I've been in these stores before." It was the first brand I'd vaguely recognized since leaving Moscow.

"Yes, it is very good." He turned into the covered parking lot and the snow finally stopped slapping against the windscreen.

"So what are we looking for today?" I asked as he found a space and pulled to a halt.

"New seats for the living area."

"What, like a couch?"

"Yes, new couch and a new big chair for my father. He needs a straight back to help him breathe. Also a new table and some book-shelves or something."

"Okay, anything else?"

"A bed for the room I sleep in. I think it is still the one I had when I was growing up. I need something else, my feet are sticking out of the end."

I laughed. "Oh dear, you should have had my bed. It's huge."

"Yes, it was bought with the house, all of the guest room furniture was because they had nothing to go in there. We've never had a guest room before." He switched off the engine and studied me. When he spoke again his voice was lower, husky even. "I wish I had been in that bed with you this week. It's driving me crazy knowing you're in there, just feet away, all warm and soft and naked and I'm not with you."

I smiled. "I haven't been sleeping naked in your parents' home."

"You would be if I was there."

"You think so, Russian boy?"

"I do." He moved closer, so close I could smell his cologne and feel the sleeve of his jacket brushing mine. "And that little stunt last night," he said, "at the dinner table, if I'd been in that bed with you later I'd have made you pay for that."

"What stunt?" I feigned shocked innocence. "There was no stunt."

He pressed his hand to the base of my neck, thumb stretched wide from his fingers, then smoothed it up the column of my throat until he cupped my chin. He smiled wickedly, as though a whole pile of dirty thoughts were romping through his mind. "You know exactly what you did, Sammy."

"No I don't." I stared into his eyes and tipped my chin.

He held my gaze. "Teasing me and making me remember fucking you. Fucking you hard against the wall and then in bed up your tight ass. You made me think of doing that, of your hot pussy around my cock, your trembling desperation for me to sink deeper, go higher, take your ass and make it mine. Make all of you mine."

My heart beat faster. His dirty words thrilled me. "You remembered that all on your own."

"No, you reminded me, and getting hard with my parents in the room is not something that is fun for me."

"Maybe it is for me."

He squeezed my cheeks, just a little. The hold was dominant and possessive and set up a chain reaction of excitement within my body. "I'd like to turn you on," he whispered. "Get your nipples hard and your juices flowing. I'd like to tease you, take you almost there, but just when you feel like your body is about to fly I'd leave you hanging." He licked his lips then brushed them over mine.

I was struggling to breathe. I wanted him to do that, all of it. Hell, my nipples were already tight and my pussy dampening. Heat traveled up my neck and my face burned.

"You'd be tied up," he said, leaning back a fraction and looking at my no doubt flushed cheeks. "Tied to the bed with black silk around your wrists so you wouldn't be able to finish yourself off. Your control would be gone, Sammy, and I don't think you'd like being teased, because you want the power, don't you?"

I couldn't deny that I wasn't embarrassed to take what I wanted when it came to sex. Power in the bedroom was something I was used to.

"You want to take what you want when you want it." He slipped his hand down my neck again, reached for the zipper on my jacket then slowly, very slowly he undid it enough so that he could slide his hand in.

He glided over my right breast, cupped it and squeezed.

I gasped as sensations shot around my chest and my nipple peaked.

"When we go to Miami," he said, his voice deep and breathy, "That is exactly what I'm going to do. We'll stay in a place with a big bed and I'll have you spread out like a cross so there is nowhere for you to hide. I'll fuck your mouth, your pussy, your ass..."

"Vadmir," I said, pressing myself into his touch. "I..."

"You want it?"

"Yes." Boy, did I ever. Except I wanted it *now*. I wanted him. "Perhaps we should forget the furniture shop and go find a hotel room."

He smiled, leaned forward and kissed me, slow but deep. As our tongues tangled he fondled my breast, tweaking my nipple through my clothing.

Eventually he pulled back, refastened the zipper on my jacket and straightened my coat. "No hotel, we have shopping to do." He pulled the keys from the ignition.

"Tease," I said with a frown.

He tipped his head back and laughed. "I haven't even started yet."

Chapter Seventeen

I spotted a long, chocolate brown sofa shaped like a large L and pointed it out to Vadmir.

"I think it is perfect," he said, dropping down on it and reading the label. "It will fill that room."

"I agree, and look, a chair that matches. Would that be okay for Ruslan?"

"I think so." He stood and then sat in it. "Mmm, yes."

I tested the sofa and stretched my legs out on it. It was firm yet comfortable and the leather could be warmed up with soft cushions and throws. It would be my first choice if I had a place of my own to furnish.

"This is good." Vadmir said. "We'll take it. Where is that pencil and paper?"

I handed it to him and he wrote the item numbers down so we could order.

"Table next?" I said, walking past several other shoppers toward a section of tables.

He followed, with his hat pulled low, and stopped by the first one I'd seen that might be suitable.

"No," he said, "too small."

"Okay, how about that one, the color matches the sofa."

"But will it match the walnut in that room?"

"Mmm, I'm not sure. Maybe go with something more contemporary, like a glass top."

"Yes, that one is nice."

"Perfect."

He walked over, smoothed his hand over the surface and then wrote down the number. As he did so I studied his fingers. It was hard to not demand he touch me again. That he put those hands on me and those fingers in me. I beat down a shiver of desire. IKEA was not the place for thinking about Vadmir exploring my body.

Next we picked out a fancy cabinet for Ruslan's hockey memorabilia then two dressing tables and stools—one each for Zoya and Darya—and a toiletry cabinet for the main bathroom.

"Bed now," Vadmir said, poking the pencil behind his ear and the paper into his jean pocket.

"Mmm, wouldn't that be nice."

He grinned and slipped his arm around my waist. "Are you still feeling teased?"

"No." I was, but not likely to admit it.

The beds were lined up in front of us. A variety of sizes, some high, some low, some with wooden headboards, some with metal. A few people were milling about, one lady was lying down, trying out a mattress for comfort.

"What do you think?" I asked, looking around. "A king size."

"Yes, the bigger the better."

"I agree."

He dropped his arm from my waist and touched the slatted wooden headboard of a large bed that had a pale, square frame. "I like this one."

"It looks okay." I sat on the edge and gave a little bounce.

"No, do it properly," he said. "Like this." He sat heavily and then swung his legs 'round and rested his head on a plastic covered pillow.

"How is it?" I asked, joining him in a supine position. The pillow rustled by my ears.

"Not bad." He turned to me and shuffled closer. "What do you think?"

"It's firm."

"Is that good?" He asked.

"It is in my book." I twisted to my side to face him. Our noses were only inches apart.

"And what about this headboard?" he asked, a naughty glint catching in his eye.

"It's very nice."

"Why?"

I glanced up at the slats. They were flat and about two inches apart. "I guess it's modern."

"And...?" He licked his lips and then tugged at the bottom one with his teeth. "What else?"

"Stylish."

He grinned. "And...?"

I hesitated. "And..."

His grin broadened. "And good for tying hot, beautiful women to who need to be taught to surrender control from time to time." He brushed the back of his index finger down my cheek. "Women like you."

God, if only I could remove everyone else in the store with one flick of a magic wand, I wouldn't hesitate. "Maybe."

"What do you mean, maybe?" He raised his eyebrows.

"Perhaps I'd like to tie you up and have my wicked way with a big, bad hockey player who thinks it's okay to prey on innocent women who are helping them shop."

"There's nothing innocent about you, Sammy." He tipped forward and pressed a kiss to my mouth.

I leaned into it and then spoke onto his lips. "Mmm, I guess not. But that doesn't mean you can get me going in the car and then drag me around IKEA."

"I like that I can turn you on. Turn you on with words and thoughts. We have some hot memories to play with."

"It would be good to make some more." I pressed my hand to his chest and slid it down to his belly. "Turn some of those thoughts into reality."

He captured my wrist and dragged it up between us. "Oh, no, not in here. I refuse to get hard in IKEA."

"I bet you're hard already."

"No." He frowned.

I raised my brows in an I-don't-believe-you expression.

"Witch," he said, then with one flick of his arm he rolled me over, onto my belly, and delivered a hard slap to my ass.

I squealed, protected my butt with my hands and scooted to the edge of the bed. "Ow, fuck, that hurt, Vadmir." As soon as my feet hit the floor I went crashing head first into a sales assistant.

"*Yest' li chto-to, chto ya mogu pomoch' vam s?*" he said, folding his arms and looking sternly between me and Vadmir.

"No, we do not need any help," Vadmir said, then appeared to remember where he was and converted back to Russian and spoke again.

The sales assistant replied with the same irritated tone as he'd spoken in previously. He frowned and gestured at me and then around the store.

Vadmir got off the mattress and rose to his full height. Slowly, deliberately, as if he had taken great offense to being spoken to in that way. He then straightened his hat and walked around the end of the bed.

The sales assistant dropped his arms, took a step back and looked up as Vadmir approached. I wasn't sure but he appeared to lose a shade of color in his face.

"He wants to know if we are purchasing this bed, so what do you think, Sammy?" Vadmir said, not taking his attention from the assistant, "shall I tell him this bed is perfect for stripping you naked, attaching you to the headboard and then doing unthinkable things to your sexy body? That I am already picturing it, already imagining you writhing in ecstasy on it?"

"You could," I said with a shrug, "or maybe explain how you'd feel if I had *you* strapped down and I was sucking your cock until you begged for mercy. I think this bed would be good for that, it's strong enough to cope with you bucking around."

He looked at me, pretended to ponder my suggestion then gave his attention to the assistant again. A long string of Russian poured from his mouth, guttural and raw and associated with hand gestures.

I loved it. Damn the man was sexy when he went all Soviet.

The assistant quickly scribbled something on a piece of paper and handed it to Vadmir.

"What did you say?" I asked.

"I told him that I would be taking the bed because the crazy American lady wants to play dirty games with me and I think it will stand up to her wild demands of my body."

My mouth fell open. "You didn't?"

He shrugged. "Honesty is the best programme."

"Policy," I said, "honesty is the best policy and not in every case."

He laughed. "Come on, we have finished shopping now. He has written down the item number, we will go and collect our furniture."

He took my hand and tugged me along. My cheeks were hot and my heart racing. I glanced over my shoulder at the member of staff. He was standing by his workstation fiddling with a pencil. He was also staring at me, watching us leave.

What the hell had Vadmir said to him?

Probably what he'd told me he had.

The journey back to Sokol was long and the car stuffed full of flat-packed furniture. One lengthy box was slotted between our seats and I had to hold it when we went 'round corners.

"This will take a lot of time to make," Vadmir said, turning the heater down. "Probably the rest of today."

"Well, I don't think we'd go out again, not in this storm."

The wipers were on full and it was also getting dark.

"I hope it stops before tomorrow," I said, "before I go back to Moscow."

"It is okay. I will take you."

"No, you mustn't. I'll get a cab."

"No, Sammy. I brought you here. I will take you back." He took his eyes from the road, briefly, to look at me. "To Moscow."

"But it's wasting a whole day with your family. Please, you've let me stay with you, let me at least get myself back to the airport. I'd hate to take you away for all of those hours. It's time you could be with your father."

He was quiet for a few moments, then. "But I—"

"No," I interrupted. "Please. If you could order me the cab, then I'd be very grateful. Or perhaps Darya will speak on the phone for me."

"I can do it."

"Thank you."

He pulled up at the apartment, right outside the front entrance and put his hazard lights on. We battled with the wind and the snow and grabbed a box each from the trunk. Mine was long and skinny, his heavy and wide. We were damp by the time we made it to the elevator but still bustled inside with our boxes. We'd have to make several trips to get all of the furniture up to the apartment.

"Damn, it's cold out there," I said, leaning my box against the wall and hitting the top floor button. My cheeks were wind bitten just from a few seconds outside.

The doors slid shut and the light dimmed to a soft golden glow.

"It's been colder," Vadmir said, propping his box next to mine and then snuggling in behind me. He wrapped his arms around my waist and buried his face in the curve of my neck. "Or maybe it just feels warmer when you're here, Sammy."

I pressed one hand over his forearm and with the other reached up and touched his cap. "I'm glad you think so."

His breath was warm, seeping around the collar of my coat, yet his nose was cool, just touching my ear.

"I have enjoyed you here."

"I've enjoyed it, too." As I said it I realized just how much I had. It had been an unusual week, and certainly not what I'd planned. But being part of the Arefyev family had been fun. They were great hosts, plus spending time with Vadmir, even if it had been clothed time, was special.

"We will see each other again, back in Orlando," he said, "won't we?"

"I'd like that." The thought of it all being over tomorrow between us was horrible. Something I couldn't contemplate.

"Good." He pulled me closer, so that his groin lodged against my ass. As usual his body was firm and solid against mine. He made me feel safe and adored and I loved that about being in his presence.

He released a small groan and squeezed us tighter together.

"Russian boy," I said quietly.

He kissed my neck and I leaned my head sideways to give him better access. The soft touch of his lips was sending tingles over my skin that shimmied down my spine. It was another tease I was sure, but being close was satisfying in itself.

"Mmm?" he asked. "What?"

"I like you doing that," I managed, because I'd forgotten what I was going to say.

"I'd like to do so much more, Sammy. I would like to really show you how much I enjoy being with you."

"And I—"

My sentence was cut off as the elevator doors swooshed open. Harsh light flooded in and the outline of another person filled my vision.

Alena.

She was staring at us. She wore the same pale brown coat and hat she'd had on at the rink yesterday, though this time she didn't look angry, she looked shocked.

Her eyes were wide and her mouth drooped open. Her arms hung at her sides with a purse loosely held in her right hand.

"Alena," Vadmir said, suddenly releasing me.

Quickly I straightened my collar and reached for my box.

Alena clamped her lips together and stepped aside. Her gaze flitted from me to Vadmir.

I exited the elevator. I'd let Vadmir sort this one out. It wasn't my problem.

"*Chto ty delayesh' zdes'?*" Vadmir said.

"*Ya prishel, chtoby uvidet' Darya,*" she replied.

He nodded, picked up his box and stepped past her. "*Do svidaniya, Alena.*"

Alena didn't reply. Her heels clacked noisily as she entered the elevator and stabbed at the button with a gloved finger.

My heart was thumping. For some reason I felt guilty. She and Vadmir had been together for years. They'd been serious, very serious, yet here I was messing around with him in her hometown. But hell, he'd invited me here and there was nothing between them anymore. She'd made her choice and it wasn't Vadmir. He was a free agent, the same as I was. We were doing nothing wrong. Quickly I squashed down my guilty emotion. I wouldn't allow it room to hold my thoughts hostage.

"I am sorry about that," Vadmir said when the elevator door shut and the whirring of the mechanics hummed around the top floor lobby.

"It's not your fault."

"She and Darya were good friends, they would have enjoyed being related by marriage."

I nodded.

"But it wasn't to be and it is crazy if they are still thinking it might happen."

"Do you think they are?" That thought did disturb me. It didn't make me feel guilty, it made me feel possessive. The thought of Vadmir marrying Alena now twisted my guts. Not that I wanted to marry him, I just didn't want him off the market, not until we'd explored whatever it was we had going on.

"No. It's old news." He opened the apartment door and lugged in both his and my box. "You wait here, I'll grab the rest of the stuff."

"No, I'll help."

He smiled and touched his lips to my cheek. "You've done enough, and also, I don't think I can trust myself in the elevator with you. It's the only place I've had you alone all day."

As we'd predicted, the entire evening was spent assembling furniture. The sofa, bed and chair were being delivered after the weekend, but the dressing tables and cabinets were a job for Vadmir and I.

Darya gave me a kiss and a hug when I'd gone into the kitchen. I couldn't help but wonder if she felt awkward that Alena had been there. But the visit wasn't mentioned and she'd gone back to making dumplings. We paused briefly to eat, then continued with our screwing and hammering, perusal of instructions—of which I could only go by the pictures—and then tightening and admiring.

Ruslan was thrilled with his new cabinet for his hockey memorabilia and I polished all of his knickknacks as he watched a hockey game and chatted to me in Russian like I understood every word.

I nodded and smiled and carefully lined up his collection of pucks and then buffed the trophies and set them inside the cabinet.

"That looks cool," Vadmir said, coming into his father's bedroom to regard my finished work.

"Yes," Darya said, smiling and passing her father a hot drink. "You are very kind to my father, Samantha. I am very grateful."

I smiled at her. "It didn't take long." She caught my eye and I was thrilled to see affection there. Perhaps we, too, would be good friends, the same as her and Alena had been. "And yes, it is nice," I said. "Vadmir chose it."

"I did have the help of an excellent assistant and expert shopper." He winked at me.

I grinned. "I'm glad you think so." I stifled a yawn. "But that's me all shopped out for one day. I'm going to hit my bed."

Vadmir nodded and something passed over his eyes, I wasn't sure what. Maybe, like me, he was sad that our last day together was over.

After a flurry of goodnights to Ruslan and Darya, I headed toward my room. I'd gone from having fun, feeling high and part of something to having a long journey and then work stretching before me. A tug of sadness pulled at my heart.

"Samantha," Zoya bustled toward me. "*Spokoynoy nochi.*"

"*Spokoynoy nochi,*" I said then repeated it in English. "Goodnight."

"Goodnight," she said with a smile that revealed a missing side tooth. She then kissed me three times, on my cheeks, as she had every night I'd been in her home.

Chapter Eighteen

I felt dusty and sweaty from all the manual work of the evening, so I had a quick shower and then fell into bed smelling of geranium and camomile. Again I was grateful for the receptionist who'd had such great taste in toiletries and clothes.

Snuggling under the duvet, I picked up my Kindle. The wind was still howling outside and sweeping around the wall my bed was against. Occasionally it gusted extra hard and the window rattled as though the wind was knocking against it, trying to come in. But I was warm and cozy so it didn't disturb me too much.

I was reading a good book and I kept on going, chapter after chapter, even though my eyes grew heavy. The apartment went quiet and I guessed everyone had retired for the night. I'd just read this last bit, one more scene.

Eventually I finished the entire novel and, glancing at the time, saw I'd read for nearly two hours. I yawned, flicked off my light and tucked the duvet in around my shoulders, ready for my last sleep in Sokol.

A small click caught my attention.

The bedroom door was opening. The weak light from the corridor highlighting a hand, an arm and then a huge silhouette.

Vadmir.

Silently he stepped in and shut the door.

"What are you doing?" I whispered.

"Shh," he said as he came toward me.

With the help of the green-tinged light of the small digital clock I could see he wore only tight black boxers.

He flicked back the duvet, letting in a waft of cool air and then the bed dipped as he climbed in beside me.

"What are you doing?" I asked again.

"I need to be with you," he said, gathering me close and winding his legs with mine. The hairs on his shins tickled mine. "Is that okay?"

"But your mother, she'll—"

"She won't find out." He curled his arm beneath me so he was holding me against his bare chest. "Not if we're quiet."

"Are you sure she doesn't have CCTV out there? Every time we've so much as kissed she's appeared."

"She's asleep, it's past midnight. Nothing wakes her between midnight and six."

"I hope you're right." I wound my arms around him. His skin was warm and smooth and smelled of his usual woodsy shower gel. "I'd hate her to think I was taking advantage of her son."

"Are you?" he asked against my lips.

"I guess I might, now that you're here." All the earlier feelings of lust came swarming back into my body. I'd wanted him for days, more than a kiss and a cuddle I'd wanted him naked, at my side. I'd wanted him inside me, I'd wanted to give him pleasure, hear him come.

"At the forest," he said, kissing over my cheek and then speaking quietly into my ear. "You made me feel amazing but you, you didn't come."

"I enjoyed it, though." I caressed his back, drawing small circles with my fingertips that explored every dip and rise of his spine. "Very much."

"Mmm, but now it is your turn to feel pleasure. But you'll have to be silent. No banging against the wall, no screaming like you usually do."

"I don't scream." I tried to be indignant but it was hard, because it was true, I was very vocal about my pleasure.

"Oh, you do and you know it. You scream, you shout, you wail, but I'm not complaining," he said. "Then I know I'm getting it right. But tonight, you need to hold that in no matter how right I get it."

"Okay." My heart was racing at the thought of finally getting some relief from the sexual tension that had been dancing between us for days.

He shifted and then tugged at the soft nightdress I was wearing. "Lose this."

I assisted him in its removal and then shoved at my panties.

"These have to go," I said, plucking at the elastic waistband of his boxers.

"No, I'm going to give you pleasure, taste you, lick you."

"But Vadmir I want you. This is our last night…"

"It's not our last night together."

"I hope not." I stroked over his short hair, a feeling of possession gripping me again. I wanted him for more than just tonight. I wanted more plans in the future with him. More time with him.

"We have Miami," he said. "We will go together and I will do all of those things I promised to do." He paused and I sensed him smiling as he kissed down my neck to my collarbone. "Dirty, bad things that will make you scream so loud I may have to gag you."

A gag was both scary and thrilling. As was the thought of the black silk he'd threatened to tie me up with earlier. I liked the whole image, the entire scene he'd built in my mind. It made me wet just thinking about lying sacrificial before Vadmir and allowing him to do with me as he wished. It wasn't a feeling I'd had before with a man but he'd brought that fantasy to life within me by describing it so vividly. "Are you a man who keeps his promise?"

"Yeah, I always keep my promise." He moved upward and looked down at my face. "Always."

"Good." Again I shoved at his boxers, this time he didn't stop me and soon they were off. "I'll hold you to it."

I cuddled nearer to him. His cock was rigid, butting into my thigh, and his flesh was hot against mine. I found his mouth and kissed him. He kissed me back, exploring my body as he did so, massaging my breasts gently and then tracing a line down my belly and between my legs.

I parted my thighs and he delved between my folds, searching out my entrance. When he pushed in, his fingers stretching me, I gasped and broke our kiss. "Vadmir."

"Shh," he said, covering my mouth with his again.

"Mmm." I spread my legs wider and he added another finger, hooked them forward and found my G-spot. Oh God, how was I going to keep quiet? He was such an accurate aim when it came to finding the places that got me going.

He set up a slow, languid rhythm, fucking me with his hand. He was building up the pressure over my clit and within me. He kissed me as though savoring the shape of my mouth and the taste of my tongue.

I arched into him and gripped his arms, feeling the solid muscle beneath.

Eventually I ended the kiss. It was getting hard to catch my breath. "Please, Vadmir, I want to come with you in me. I'll be quiet, I swear."

"I don't know if I can trust myself," he said, also a little breathless. "To not get carried away and fuck you hard."

"You can, please, I know you can." I knew I was begging but I didn't care. The cock nudging at my hip needed to be inside my pussy...now.

I wriggled and dislodged his fingers.

He kind of growled and gripped my waist, pulling me closer.

"My purse," I said, "next to the lamp. There's a condom in the side pocket."

He stilled.

For a moment I didn't think he was going to get it. I thought he might leave. But then he reached for my purse and found the condom.

"Sammy, I..." he said.

"What?"

He sat back, rolled the condom on and then loomed over me.

I pulled the duvet up his back to his shoulders, keeping us both cocooned within its warmth.

"What, Vadmir?" I asked again.

He supported his weight on his elbows and his face hovered above mine. I stretched my legs apart, preparing to take him in.

"You are one of the most beautiful people I have ever met," he said. "You have been so kind with my family and me. I will never forget this, ever."

Our mouths connected and his cock found my entrance.

I gripped his outer thighs with my knees and grasped his tense buttocks as he slid to full depth.

I wanted to moan and gasp and tell him how great he felt, but as he'd asked me to I held it in. My chest tightened with the effort of reining in that groan of delight.

He buried to the hilt and we both stilled. I could feel his balls pressing up against my ass cheeks, his wide cock stretching my internal muscles and his pecs pressing against my breasts.

I squirmed, allowing a little fizz of pleasure to hum through my clit. He was so dense above me. He'd become my world, for that moment in time there was only him; me and him.

He withdrew almost out and then eased back in. It had felt great the first time he'd plunged in, but now it was amazing. He'd rubbed my clit with his hard body and all the tension that was looking for release had bubbled up to the surface.

"Vadmir, oh, yes," I gasped, tearing my lips from his. "Yes."

"Shh." He did it again. Pulled out and then slowly rode back in.

"Ah, yeah, fuck, just like that I—"

He clamped his hand over my mouth.

I stared up at him. A whimper caught in my throat.

"You cannot be trusted," he said.

He was right. I couldn't. I wanted to wail and shout, demand more, faster, harder. It was probably best that he silenced me this way.

He continued to fuck me in a slow, languid ride. He was in no rush, but that was fine because neither was I. Trouble was my body had other ideas and before I knew it my orgasm was there. The point of no return was reached and I bucked and shook, driving my hips down onto him to maximize the depth of his cock and then clawing at his back.

"Fuck you feel amazing when you hug my cock with your pussy," he said, stretching his head to the ceiling and the tendons in his neck elongating. "I love it when you come like this."

I couldn't reply, he was still keeping me quiet with his hand clasped tight over my mouth. But I watched as his face contorted, his teeth gritted and he squeezed his eyes shut.

With one powerful shunt that created a single squeak on the bedframe, he came. He flooded the condom with his heated pleasure, his shaft spasming in my pussy and his balls mashing up against me.

He looked spectacular in the throes of ecstasy. More gorgeous than I'd ever seen a man.

Fuck I wanted him. I wanted him again. I wanted him again soon.

He dragged in several deep breaths and a full body tremble shook its way down his body from his shoulders to his legs. "Ah, yeah," he said on a gasp. "So good." He looked back down at me, his eyes glistening. "Can I move my hand?" he asked, his voice low and hoarse.

I nodded.

"You won't scream?"

I shook my head.

He lifted his hand and kissed me. I wound my arms around his neck and hugged him close. Trying to let him know with that kiss how special our lovemaking had been. It was more than fucking. It was being together, connecting. When I'd first met him it had been all about what fun I could have with his sexy body. Now there was more, now I knew the man. I knew he was kind and caring and seemed to really like me for me. Not just my looks or my clothes but me, inside.

"*Milaya moya*, you're so good for me," he said. "I feel alive when I'm in you. The only other time I feel like that is when I'm on the ice."

"You're good for me, too." I stroked his cheek and the angle of his jaw and chin, committing it all to memory. "What does *Milaya moya* mean?"

"My sweetheart."

He reached down, secured the end of the condom and then withdrew.

I missed him instantly, his cock, his weight over me and his hips pressing my legs wide.

Quickly he sorted the condom then lay back down and scooped me close. "I'll stay until five, then I will sneak out."

"Don't oversleep. We have a habit of doing that."

"I won't." He kissed my temple. "Don't worry."

I closed my eyes and felt him rest his chin on the top of my head. It felt so right to have my face buried in his neck, smelling him and sharing his body heat. The sound of the wind faded and in its place the sound of Vadmir's breathing and the steady drumming of his heartbeat filled my ears.

I sighed, pressed up close, and let sleep carry me away.

* * * *

I woke alone the next morning. It seemed Vadmir had managed to wake at five and sneak back into his own bedroom without discovery. All was calm and as it usually was.

Darya made a breakfast of pancakes and jam, assuring me it was good for the ride to Moscow. She then headed out to work saying that she'd see me before I went at lunchtime.

I showered and dressed, then packed my bag. I had a couple of hours to wait before my cab and sat with Ruslan and Vadmir, who were watching a documentary on the sports channel about a new Viper player called Mateus Blanc who was performing well in the playoffs. He was

Canadian, the programme was in English yet had Russian subtitles, and I was quite happy to stare at it without really watching.

Eventually the time came for me to depart. I kissed Ruslan good-bye. He had tears in his eyes and held my hands so tightly I didn't think he'd ever let go. Darya came back on her lunch break just as Zoya was hugging the breath from me.

"Oh, Samantha, we're going to miss you," Darya said, removing her mother's arms from around my neck. "It's been so nice having you stay. I love having another girl about the place."

"I'll miss you, too," I said, giving her a hug. "And when I get my next lease organized, you must come over to Florida and stay."

"I can come and stay with Vadmir anytime," she said. "As long as my parents are well enough to manage without me."

"Oh, yes, of course. Well, come soon and I'll take you shopping. Show you the best places for designer bargains."

"I'd love that." She kissed me on my cheeks, three times, and then allowed Vadmir to steer me out of the apartment. I saw her pull a tissue from her sleeve and wipe her eyes. I felt the same sadness. It was hard to leave.

We traveled down in the elevator in silence. I stared at our blurred reflection in the steel door. We looked so right together, now that I saw us side by side again, we worked perfectly.

As the doors opened he pulled in a long low breath and sighed. Suddenly he didn't look so big.

"It's here," I said, pointing to the cab that was sitting with its engine running just outside of the entrance. "Waiting."

"Yes." He placed my holdall, which he'd been carrying, onto the tiled floor and rubbed his fingers over his temples.

"What's the matter?" I reached out, smoothed the collar on the fleecy shirt he wore and then rested my hand on his chest.

"I wish you were staying." He looked at his feet and shifted in his sneakers. "I like having you with me. I liked having you in my arms last night."

I quashed down the prickling feeling in my lower eyelids. "I wish I was, too, but I must go back to work, earn a living."

"Will you always do this, airline work?"

"I don't know. It suits me for now."

"Is it dangerous? Always being in the air?"

"No, it's one of the safest places to be."

He wrapped his arms around me and pulled me close. I bunched his shirt in my fist and hung onto it. It was a bittersweet moment. Much as I loved being in his arms the fact it was a parting embrace gave it a sting.

"I will call you," he said, "now that you have put your number in my phone. When I get back to Orlando in one week, I will call you."

"Yes, that would be nice."

"We will go to *Ciao* for pasta and Miami for fun and, if you want, I'll take you to the movies, too."

"I'd like that."

He dipped his head, pulled me upward onto my toes and kissed me goodbye.

Chapter Nineteen

Two weeks later

My feet throbbed and my eyes felt like they'd been rubbed with grit. It had been a long haul back from Moscow with a three-hour delay in New York City.

Harmony and I had found a new apartment—a nice place in a gated community and with a municipal pool—and I wandered in and dropped my purse on the sofa. No need for IKEA shopping, it had come fully furnished.

I was glad to be alone. Harmony was spending time with family, leaving the apartment silent and still. It was just what I needed. Being sociable wasn't high on my priority list right now and it had taken all of my energy to be polite to the passengers—pasting on my work smile had taken more effort than it usually did.

Vadmir had journeyed back from Moscow the previous week. His flight had been crewed by the opposite shift so our paths hadn't crossed. But I knew he'd arrived in Florida seven days ago, that he'd had his usual first class seat and there'd been no delays.

I kicked off my shoes and ran a bath, tipping an entire bottle of spiced apple foam into the cascading water. I ached all over, inside and out. I didn't think it was possible to actually have physical pain from acute disappointment, but that was what had happened to me. Every time I thought of Vadmir my chest ached and it became an effort to breathe.

He hadn't called. He'd said he would, as soon as he arrived in Orlando, but he hadn't. We'd made plans, plans for dinner, Miami, movies. Why the hell had he said it if he hadn't meant it? Why the hell hadn't he picked up the phone?

Bastard. They were all the same, men.

I stripped, hung my uniform up and piled my hair on the top of my head. I sank into the steaming water, my limbs sagging as I rested back and let the bubbles rise up to my chin.

I didn't have Vadmir's personal number so I couldn't call him, but even if I did, my pride wouldn't allow it. No, I wouldn't go chasing some hockey player who thought he could have any woman he wanted. A man who said things he didn't follow through on. It was just as well I'd taken what I'd needed from his hot body when I'd had the chance.

Closing my eyes, I sighed. Memories of us together besieged me. Whenever I had a quiet moment. I could picture him—his handsome, angled face laughing, teasing, frowning...coming. I could hear him, that raw, mysterious language of his that seemed to rumble up from his chest and did funny, fluttery things to my belly. I'd adored the way he whispered to me, his breath hot on my cheek and his words full of sinful suggestions. Sometimes I could even taste him, smell him, and it didn't take much for me to remember his touch, the way he could make me feel, the way he could make me come.

Tears formed behind my closed lids, escaped and trickled down my cheeks. I hated myself for crying over a man I'd known for such a short space of time. That I was so weak I'd let myself fall for charm and good looks. It wasn't who I was. I was Samantha Headington, glamorous, independent woman of the world. Men didn't get to me, especially not full-of-themselves hockey players who broke promises.

Hockey.

An idea formed in my mind. I wanted to see Vadmir but I didn't want him to see me. I needed to remind myself what he looked like. Sure I could Google him, online there were plenty of pictures of him on and off the ice, but I needed to see him in action. See if he was still the same person I thought I knew and make sure he really was back in the country and it wasn't some imposter. Maybe I'd see him and instantly understand why he hadn't called.

I'd get myself a ticket to a Vipers game. Yes, that was what I'd do. I'd sit hidden in the audience somewhere and watch him do his stuff. Hockey was of little interest to me and I was sure once I saw him, doing his job, it would put things straight in my mind. We weren't meant to be together. We were too different. That was just how it was. I should move on, I *would* move on. Perhaps I'd even see if I could switch flights so I didn't have to listen to passengers speaking Russian anymore, because that just reminded me of him. Memories of him hurt, they were too acute.

After drying and pulling on Calvin Klein sweats and t-shirt, I went onto the Viper homepage to find out when their next game was. Luckily it was the following evening, I wasn't due to fly until the day after and it was a home fixture. Perfect. I'd strike while the idea was still fresh in my mind.

I didn't have a season ticket so I had to call the box office hotline. It took a bit of time but eventually I had a seat in the home crowd, one at the back, but that suited me just fine. All I had to do now was get through it, then I could wash my hands of Vadmir Arefyev, slot him into the ancient history file in my heart and put it all down to experience. I wouldn't be dating dumb jocks again. That was one thing I was sure of.

The sun beat down on the outer skin of the Vipers' rink, the glare of the red paint dazzling in the evening light. I'd worn jeans and I had a jacket with me. But outside I could already feel perspiration tickling my armpits and cleavage. I knew, though, that once inside it would be cool. Hopefully not as cold as the Sokol rink, because that had been positively frosty. Even more so when Alena had arrived and treated me to her Medusa stare.

As I walked in and took my seat, neatly tucked high at the back with no danger of being recognized by anyone on ground level, I thought of Alena. She'd been beautiful and wounded. Much as she'd been furious and upset that first time I'd seen her talking to Vadmir, the second time we'd met, at the apartment, she'd looked shocked to the bones, as if her world had fallen apart. The elevator door had opened and she'd seen the man she loved—which I presumed she did as her reaction to me was so intense—with another woman. If that had been me the earth would have shifted, my heart would have broken in two and I would have felt sick to my guts. It had happened in my life, once. I had loved someone who didn't love me. He'd loved another and was happy to string me along as a plaything for months. But that was years ago and it hadn't happened again since. I wouldn't allow it to.

A drum roll suddenly boomed around the stadium. The lights dipped and spotlights flashed over the ice highlighting the blue and red lines in a frenzied display. The fans went wild, screaming and shouting. My ears rang with the noise of it. The mascot, an awkward looking alligator, raced around the edge throwing candy over the Plexi and creating even more turmoil.

I yanked the zipper on my jacket up to my chin and pulled the black beanie I wore lower over my ears. The drum switched to rap music, Eminem I thought—shout-singing about pumping it up and going down. The crowd clapped in time to the beat. The man in front of me repeatedly punched the air.

The players streaked onto the ice. Like arrows releasing from a bow the home team dominated the rink. Flashes of red and white, they held their sticks high and waved to the crowd, completing a super-fast lap of honor.

I strained to see over the man in front of me who now had both arms held aloft and was waving frantically. I could just about make out the names on the back of the players' jerseys printed in bold black lettering. It was impossible to see faces clearly, they had helmets on with visors and I was too far away.

The opposition raced on in blue and green, the Canucks, and spread out around the stadium. I spotted Lewis, the team captain, speaking to a ref and then dashing off to converse with a couple of players including the goalkeeper.

He turned, the goalkeeper, and adjusted his bulky padding, giving me chance to read his name. Reed. So it wasn't Harmony's night of fun playing today after all.

The music came to an end but the crowd still roared. It was as if they were impatient for the game to start and they couldn't wait another moment.

But there seemed to be some issue that Lewis wasn't happy with and waiting was the only option for the fans. He'd skated over to the boards and was talking with a coach who was nodding furiously.

I glanced up at an enormous screen that had previously been showing past Viper goals. It was now running through player stats. I didn't even have time to read any of Logan Taylor's details when Vadmir Arefyev's face filled the screen.

My breath lodged in my throat. I clenched my fists and shoved them into my pockets. Seeing his face, huge like that, and with a mean, determined expression had caught me off guard. Sure I'd come here to see him, but...

I didn't read the details of his height and weight and number of Vipers games he'd played and points he'd scored. I just looked at those ice blue eyes, eyes I thought I'd known so well, eyes that had gazed at me full of lust, teasing and affection.

I swallowed, tore my gaze away and checked out the action on the rink.

Play was finally about to start.

The puck dropped. Lewis was first to claim possession, snatching it away from a Canuck and then turning his back on him and racing toward the left wing. He passed it on and then received it back in the hook of his stick.

Already I was struggling to keep up with the little black disc. The Vipers shot it between themselves so quickly, always evading the opposition and tapping it left to right as they moved.

The player closest to me had the puck trapped up against the boards, a Canuck tried to steal it but the Viper sent it safely up the wing. Another caught it but he was rammed in the chest and crushed into the Plexi. The name Arefyev splattered up against the clear barrier.

I gasped and clasped my hands to my mouth. The entire length of the rink had shook with the power of that barge. Surely that must have done some serious damage to Vadmir. Would the ref stop play?

No, and it seemed it hadn't done him any damage. I thought he might collapse, need medics, but Vadmir simply shoved at his opponent, shoulder-charged him out of the way then shot the puck to Taylor who was waiting in the center.

My attention was glued on Vadmir now. He was all I could look at, all I wanted to watch. The puck was no longer of interest to me. He hung around the goal, protecting it, a layer of defense between center ice and Reed. He skated backward as quickly as he went forward, often taking the puck behind the goal and then shooting it back up the wing, always with absolute precision and lightning-fast skill.

"Neat backhand," the man in front shouted to his neighbor when Vadmir sent the puck shooting left and it was passed to the center.

"Yeah, thank fuck Arefyev is on ice again," came the reply. "Really fucking missed him keeping danger out of the zone."

I'd missed him, too. More than I wanted to admit because that squeezed my heart.

The game continued, but instead of keeping up I stared at the way Vadmir's jersey hung off his wide shoulders; shoulders I'd gripped, scratched my nails down and had had my thighs wrapped around. A tremble shivered between my legs. He was so damn sexy. If I'd thought coming here would put me off him I'd been mistaken.

He didn't move, he glided. Darting away from anyone that came close and sneaking in and stealing the puck when it headed his way. He stopped a goal that looked so certain the Canuck fans were already on their feet. Viper fans went wild, chanting his name, clapping their hands. He was their hero.

He gave one brief acknowledgment of this, turning my way and raising his stick in the air then he was all business again, head down, doing his stuff.

I caught my breath, even though I knew he wouldn't see me in a crowd of hundreds, for a brief moment his face had raised to look at the stands.

I sat down with a bump, hiding behind the man in front. Prickles of heat swarmed over my head, making my scalp itch against my beanie hat.

"Fuck, off-side, off-side," shouted someone to my right.

I peered down at the game again. An ice battle had resumed. It seemed three Vipers had got into an altercation with a couple of Canucks and they were all shoving at each other. I searched for Vadmir but he was at the opposite end of the rink, back stooped, stick low, just waiting.

"Yeah, knock him out," I heard someone shout.

The fight was heating up. One Viper was on the floor, another was locked in an arm-grip with a Canuck, twisting and turning on the ice and trying to keep their balance as they tussled and tugged at each other's jerseys. The Canuck tried to land a punch and failed, and the Viper, who I could now see was Taylor, successfully struck his aggressor's helmet with a gloved hand. A linesman raced up, whistle in his mouth, but he got too close and was knocked to the ice.

Eminem music started up again, loud and piercing. The crowd erupted, they were alive and loving the fight that had broken out. It didn't end, they kept on going, bashing against the boards, more players piling in.

Vadmir held back. I kept glancing at him to see what he'd do. Some players, who were waiting behind the boards had their legs over, desperate to join in the ruckus. Coaches were shouting, cameras were flashing.

"Go, go, go," the men in front of me chanted, punctuating the air with each word.

Suddenly, as quickly as it started, the fight was over. The music stopped and play resumed. Vadmir got a quick touch of the puck and then shot it to Taylor, who still looked disheveled. Taylor did a twist and a turn around three Canucks and then slid the puck home.

The crowd around me burst upward, screaming and yelling in delight. I couldn't help standing and clapping, too. The joy was infectious.

The lights dimmed, the spots streaked over the ice and wild electric music filled the arena. The screeching beaty rhythm vibrated from my soles through my body.

Vadmir slid up to the goalkeeper and they high-fived.

I found myself beaming. Pleased for him. Pleased for the Vipers. It seemed I had a hockey team now.

Damn it! I wasn't even interested in hockey.

The game ended five-three. Vipers had won. As I wandered outside amid the swarm of fans their joy was electric. Mine, however, was sapping away. I'd done what I'd set out to achieve, seen the man I thought I'd started a relationship with. But it had left me hollow. If I'd thought seeing him would help I was wrong. Now I was even more convinced that what I'd lost had been something special. *He* was something special.

But now it was over and I'd never see him again.

Chapter Twenty

"Crew seats for takeoff," Captain Marks announced on the tannoy as we taxied toward the runway. The engines rumbled louder, the pilot was making up time. We were late departing.

I sat next to Harmony, buckled up, and glanced out of the window. Outside the sun was beating down on the tarmac and shimmering in long waves of heat.

"You okay?" Harmony asked.

"Fine. Just tired."

"Me too, and fat. My family, I swear, eat more than normal people. Who needs six choices of pudding after dinner? It's impossible to not sample everything." She rubbed her stomach. "Still, it makes up for not eating for a week after those damn shrimp."

"Have you heard from Jackson?" I asked.

"No, we didn't swap numbers. It was just a night of wild fucking." She shrugged and I wished I could have her flippant attitude to time spent with a sexy hockey player.

"What about you," she asked. "Have you heard from him?"

I shook my head. I'd finally told Harmony all about Vadmir and our week together. I'd had no choice. She'd guessed something had happened in Russia and soon connected the two. But it was good that she knew. I needed my best friend's support while I was so low.

The plane took a tight corner and lurched to the right.

"Jesus, Captain Speed Demon is putting his foot down." Harmony gripped the seat.

I held my safety belt and wished I was at home in bed. I didn't feel like working today. I should have called in sick.

The engines roared and the plane kicked up the gears, pressing me into my chair. It tipped to the right then the left, the whole fuselage rocking.

"Windy out there," Harmony said.

"Yes. Should get us there quickly, though, make up the lost time."

"Means we'll have to be fast with lunch."

"Yes."

We hurtled along, rattling over the runway. The engines blasted out energy. The plane tipped again, to the left then to the left a bit more.

My stomach lurched. A bad taste formed in my mouth. Something wasn't right.

But still we shot along. I waited for the nose to tip upward, for the plane to lift from the ground. Out of the window I could see the terminal getting smaller and smaller. Shrinking into the distance.

"Fuck," Harmony muttered. "What's he doing?"

"I don't know." I glanced at her. She had the same flash of fear in her eyes that I knew was in mine. It took a lot to rattle an air stewardess but adrenaline was now pumping into my system.

I shook my head, just a fraction, and reached for the St. Christopher around my neck. I rubbed it between my index finger and thumb. The engines were screaming. The plane felt unstable, as though it was too heavy for the thrust but too light for the wind buffeting it around.

Suddenly the brakes came on. I was plunged forward, as was Harmony. Our safety belts trapped us against the seats and knocked the breath from my lungs.

A chorus of screams rang out—passengers terrified by the sudden violent deceleration.

I stared at everyone's heads bobbing about. The sound of the plane skidding on the tarmac screeched around my brain. The plane shook, juddered, and the seats rattled. Several overhead compartments flew open, contents spilling out and landing on the people below.

"Shit," Harmony gasped.

Another violent jerk had me lifting out of my seat. My limbs flew upward and then crashed back down, my spine shrieked in complaint as a shard of pain raced through it. My body was out of control, I couldn't stop it being battered and flung around.

Harmony yelped next to me, her head cracking on the back of the seat.

Our speed didn't seem to be reducing. Terror gripped me. The sounds of the passengers crying out, yelling, screeching was partially drowned by the booming sounds of the plane crashing.

Shit. We were crashing. Something had gone terribly wrong.

Suddenly instinct kicked in. All of those hours and hours of training came to the front of my mind. This was my job, much as being a mile-high waitress was part of my role, staying cool when everyone around me panicked was also what I needed to do. And this was the real deal. Now. We all hoped we'd never have to use the skills we'd had drummed into us but if we did, then there was nothing else for it but to do our stuff.

The safety belt pinched against my hips, struggling to hold me against the seat. The plane tipped to the left, renewing the sharp pain in my back again. An almighty bang told me the wing was on the tarmac. We began to spin. Flying forward and hurtling 'round in a doughnut.

I shut my eyes and clenched my teeth. Wondered if death would be quick. A picture of Vadmir reaching for me, his big strong arms wrapping around me, hovered in my mind's eye. I suppressed a sob. I really would never see him again. Never hear his voice or see his smile.

"Fire," Harmony gasped.

I flicked open my eyes. Sniffed the air. She was right, there was a whiff of smoke, electrical, seeping toward us.

"We're stopping," she said. "I think."

I looked out of the window. My neck struggled to cope with the turbulent skid we appeared to be stuck in. We did, however, appear to be slowing.

"We have to get everyone out, quick," I said, reaching for my buckle.

She clasped her hand over mine, stretching downward because the way the plane was now slanted to the left. "Wait," she said.

She was right, we were still moving fast. But with each passing second we slowed.

Finally, we came to a halt. Instantly I was standing, hauling myself upright with the help of the seat in front of me. I ignored the spasm-like pain in my back.

The main lights were off and, despite it being mid-morning, the fuselage was dark, dark and a boiling mass of confusion. I lunged for the exit, rammed the safety off and flung it open. The smell of smoke hit me as a puff of black air wafted past the door. An almighty whack and a bright flash of yellow unfolded, the slide deploying from the bustle.

I could hear the emergency vehicles in the distance. Behind me Harmony barked instructions.

Hurriedly I turned back to the passengers only to be knocked out of the way by a man throwing himself at the slide. I dropped to my knees then dragged myself up again. "Your shoes," I said to a woman who was hauling herself past me wearing magnificent silver stilettoes, "take them off."

She slipped from her high heels and lunged toward the exit.

I glanced down and saw the man who'd pushed past me holding out his arms to break her slide.

"Can you stay there and help?" I shouted down to him.

"Yes!"

I turned, coughed and helped a child and his father to the exit. "Go quickly," I said. "And hold him tight." The safety lights were on, people dragging themselves through the wonky plane toward me. I secured my footing and lodged my hip against the wall, reached out and pulled passengers close and then sent them out of the exit.

Over and over I did this, bang, bang, bang getting them off the plane. Terror seared across everyone's faces. Shouts were coming from farther back in the fuselage where Patrick and his team would be doing the same as Harmony and me. A woman with blood running down her face struggled to get up. I grabbed her shoulder, pulled and then was relieved when a male passenger wrapped his arm around her waist and took her out with him.

My eyes were stinging. The smoke was getting thicker. But the plane was emptying. I could see the last passengers.

"We've got to get out of here," Harmony said, spluttering. "I can smell fuel now. It's going to blow."

"Yes," I said, "nearly done."

The emergency sirens were screeching through the air. "Are the pilots out?" Harmony shouted.

"We're here."

I turned and saw Captain Marks and his crew. Their usual immaculate appearance was ruffled and they had urgency in their expressions.

An older man was battling to reach us. I dashed toward him, holding onto the seats as I went.

"Get out, Harmony," the Captain said. "Samantha, you too."

"Hang on." I reached the man, his glasses were shattered and he appeared to have a broken wrist. His left hand was floppy and useless and he was clutching it. "Hold on to me," I said, "We'll get you out."

He grabbed me, he was heavy but I hauled him several paces.

Suddenly Captain Marks was in front of me. "Go," he said, scooping the man up and holding him against his chest. "Now."

I lunged forward. The rest of the crew were off the plane. The smoke was so dense now it was hard to see, hard to breathe. The low-level lighting lit my way, though it was disorientating being at a side angle.

I reached the exit. Captain Marks was close behind me. I glanced over my shoulder at him. He was struggling. Quickly I helped pull the old man forward. He appeared unconscious now.

"Get off the plane now, ma'am!"

I looked downward. At the base of the slide two fire officers were holding out their arms to me. Behind them were several other fire crew members unrolling hoses. It was dark and disorientating and I was light-headed from the smoke. I tried to recall everything I was supposed to do. My section was clear, everyone was out now, except for the old man.

Captain Marks stumbled and fell onto his ass, the man he was helping like a rag doll against him. "Go," I said, pushing them both to the door using my hands and my feet. "I'm right behind you."

They slid down in a tumble of arms and legs. The fire officers at the bottom helped them stop and then one threw the unconscious passenger over his shoulder and rushed away.

I pressed my arms across my chest, the way I'd been taught, and jumped onto the slide. I went fast and hurtled down. Panic rose in me. I couldn't stop—only hot, hard tarmac awaited me.

"Hey, I've got you." Big arms reached for me, then I was scooped up and pressed against a hard chest.

"Thanks," I gasped to the fire officer who'd caught me. I looked up at his face but he had the visor down on his safety helmet and I couldn't see his features just the reflection of the plane, swamped in orange flames.

He turned and began to run, carrying me with him. I gripped his jacket and sucked in oxygen as the smoke thinned.

Just ahead of me a passenger, the first man who'd got out, was rushing along. He turned, iPhone in his hand, and snapped a photograph.

* * * *

"It certainly is dramatic," Patrick said, looking at the front page of the *New York Times*.

I studied the picture again and a wave of nausea swept over me. The image of me being carried away from a burning plane by a big hunk of a fireman was splashed over nearly every newspaper in the country. My hair was whipping out behind me, my skirt ruffled up so that I was unwittingly flashing a length of my thigh, and my feet were bare. At some point I'd lost my shoes but I couldn't remember when.

"Thank goodness he carried you," Harmony said, leaning over and pointing at my feet. "You'd have burned your feet on the runway, it's completely melted."

"I know." I shuddered and the pulled muscle in my back protested at the movement. I reached into my purse for another painkiller and knocked it back with a slug of coffee. "What time is this supposed to start?" I nodded at the clock that showed eleven. Exactly twenty-four hours since the incident. I felt drained, exhausted, but also a little floaty; I guessed it was the codeine.

"Now," Patrick said, crossing his legs and stabbing the air with his foot in a jerky, impatient movement. "They'll be here any minute. Sooner the better, I just want to go home to bed."

"My head still aches," Harmony said, rubbing the back of it. "I know they said it was okay but that doesn't stop it hurting."

"Yeah, I know what you mean," I said, "I can still smell the smoke, too. It's like it's got stuck in my nose."

"And the screams," Patrick said, clasping his hand over his cheek. "I know we trained for this stuff but they don't prepare you for just how loud the screams are." He grimaced. "I'll never forget them. This one woman, she was hysterical, I thought I was going to have to slap her around the face to get her to listen to me."

The door to the conference room opened and we all went quiet—a crew of eight who'd all been to Hell the day before but luckily had come out of the other side. We were battered and bruised, none of us had had much sleep and our pale faces and tired eyes showed that.

"Ladies and gentlemen." It was Baron Taylor, Head of Safety. I'd never seen him before but heard his name many times. He was in his mid-fifties with gray hair and sharp eyes. He wore a smart navy suit and a tie with the airline emblem stamped all over it.

He strode in and took a seat in the rough circle we'd assembled our-selves in. Two more members of staff, one of them Nicola, sat either side of him.

"Good morning," he said, looking at us all.

There was a murmur of good mornings and general shuffling.

"First off," he said, "I've just heard that the gentleman, the one with the broken wrist and concussion, is doing very well this morning so that's good news to kick off with."

I nodded. I was pleased to hear that.

"It's remarkable and a credit to you folks that there weren't more in-juries, minor or worse or, Heaven forbid, fatalities." He smiled, placed his hands on his thighs and leaned forward. "I want you all to relax be-cause today is just an informal chat, a debrief. Everyone will be spoken to individually but I wanted us to gather here now and talk about the events of yesterday while it's still fresh in everyone's head." He paused. "What went well? What could have gone better? Do you have any ideas for improving evacuation policy?" He smiled. "Luckily these events are extremely rare but having experienced the situation we all train for you are now valuable commodities in assisting with the next generation of safety measures."

He looked around and gestured to our cups. "Does everyone have a drink?"

Most people nodded. He really was doing his best to put us at ease.

I shifted on the hard plastic seat and hoped the pain in my back would soon settle. I knew it was nothing serious, they'd X-rayed it at the hospital, it was muscular but still, I wouldn't be dancing or going on rollercoasters for a while. I just wanted to lie down, stretch out flat and let my body heal.

"Ah, Ms. Headington," Baron said, looking my way. "It's your pic-ture the country is waking up to."

"Yes, sir," I said.

"And how do you feel about that?"

I hesitated. I hadn't really thought much about it. I guess I was still a bit shocked from the crash. I hadn't slept much; Harmony and I had pulled duvets onto the sofa and talked most of the night, running through events as a way of sifting through our turbulent memories. "I'd have preferred to have had time to brush my hair and add some lipstick," I said with a smile.

There was a polite murmur of laughter.

Baron gave me a gentle nod. "You were the last out I've been told."

"Yes, sir." I sipped my drink.

"Captain Marks left before you."

"Only because I shoved him. He was struggling, he had the unconscious passenger to deal with, a dead weight."

"You did the right thing," Baron said, smiling. "And it was very brave of you."

I shrugged. "I was just doing my job." I pointed to the picture of me on the front cover of the paper Patrick had on his knee. "Just like this fire officer was."

"And you did your job very well," Baron said. He looked around the small group. "There are a few things I'd like to talk about, with everyone—"

An almighty bang shook the room. The door had been flung open, cracking against the wall and shifting a picture on its hook.

Filling the doorframe was a man—a big man with long thick legs, wide shoulders, short hair and an expression that screamed determination.

"Oh, fuck," Harmony gasped. "It's your Viper, Samantha."

Vadmir stepped into the room. His gaze searched the spread of faces and eventually settled on mine.

"I'm sorry, I couldn't keep him out," panted one of the office secretaries, rushing in behind him. She had a clipboard pressed to her chest and her hair had partially escaped its updo.

"It's okay," Baron said, standing. He folded his arms and looked Vadmir up and down. "Can I help you with something?"

"No," Vadmir said. He walked up to Patrick, snatched the paper from his lap and stared at the photograph. "Fuck!"

"Oh, Christ on a motorbike," Patrick said, fluttering his fingers over his legs where the newspaper had just been.

Vadmir stared at me. His brow creased and his teeth gritted. "This," he said, flashing the picture my way, "shouldn't have happened."

"What are you doing here?" I asked. My heart was fluttering and my stomach clenching. His presence when I was feeling delicate was even more overwhelming than usual. Especially when I hadn't thought I'd ever see him again.

"I have come to get you," he said, tilting his chin and tensing his jaw.

"But I..." I was already in shock, now it was doubled. "You can't come in here."

Baron stepped between me and Vadmir. "She's right, you can't come in here. We are debriefing, Mr...?"

"Arefyev." Vadmir glared at him. "Vadmir Arefyev."

"Mr. Arefyev, if you could wait outside." There was a tone of command in Baron's voice. He was clearly used to getting his own way and being obeyed without question.

"Certainly," Vadmir said. He stepped around Baron, wrapped his hand around my upper arm and pulled me to my feet. "I'll take Sammy with me."

"Ow," I said as my back twinged. "What are you doing?"

"Are you hurt?" He frowned down at me.

"A pulled muscle, in my back."

He pressed his lips together and shook his head. He looked as though he was in pain, too. "It didn't say in the paper that you were hurt." He shook it and several of the inner sheets fell out. "It says the crew were all unharmed."

"Well, yes, but I—"

"You are coming with me." He gently slipped his hand around my waist and it felt as though he'd lifted me against the side of his body.

"I can't just leave," I said.

"Yes you can." His voice had switched from hard to soft.

"This is preposterous," Baron said, taking hold of my opposite arm, as though about to tug me away from Vadmir.

Vadmir sucked in a breath. His chest expanded against my shoulder. He stared at Baron's fingers around my arm and anger flashed in his eyes.

"Oh, my…" Patrick whimpered and squirmed on his seat.

"You can't take my crew member anywhere," Baron said, then clicked his tongue against the roof of his mouth. "We are in a meeting. She stays here, with me." He pulled me toward him. "She's ours, an employee."

I winced as discomfort circled from my back to my chest. "Ouch."

Vadmir loomed over me and pushed his face up to Baron's. "Get. Off. Her," he growled, "Now."

"No, not a chance," Baron said. "Could someone please call security? This man must be removed."

"Vadmir, please," I said, feeling lightheaded.

Vadmir shot out his hand and wrapped it around Baron's wrist. His knuckles whitened. He was gripping him really hard.

Baron yelped. "Fuck, let go. This is assault."

"Are you going to let go of my woman?" Vadmir snarled.

"No, we are in a meeting…"

"You will be in a meeting your maker in a fucking minute."

"Shit, damn it, okay," Baron said, releasing my arm. "Jesus."

Vadmir released his grip on Baron, pushing him away in the process.

Baron staggered and clutched his right arm to this chest. "Assault," he said again.

"You are right, grabbing her like that was assault," Vadmir said. "And there are plenty of witnesses."

"But I—"

"Oh, be a man," Vadmir said. "She's coming with me. She shouldn't be here after what happened yesterday. Are you mad? All of these people need to be at home, recovering."

Harmony passed my purse to me. "Don't forget this."

Vadmir reached for it and then scooped me close again. I wanted to push him away, demand that he leave and get out of my workplace. But feeling him close, hearing his voice, it was a balm to my fractured nerves and I realized how much I'd wanted him last night, to hold and soothe me. I'd thought I really never would see him again when we were crashing. He would have been the last thing I'd thought about had I died on that runway.

We reached the door that he'd smacked against the wall. A security man stood blocking our way. He had a grim expression on his face and his peaked hat was pulled low.

Vadmir stopped in front of him. He was easily a head taller than the security guy.

"You are not going to try and stop me, are you?" Vadmir said in a low, dangerous voice. "Because I wouldn't want you to get hurt."

"No." The security guard stepped to one side. "I just need to make sure you leave." He glanced at me. "Miss?"

"Yes, I'm leaving with him."

Chapter Twenty-One

Vadmir helped me to the lot and into his car. He carefully buckled my belt and set my purse on my lap.

My head was spinning. A combination of shock and codeine. Everything I looked at had a hazy outline.

"Where are we going?" I asked when he started driving.

"To my place."

I rested my head back. "No, take me home. You can't just waltz back into my life and snatch me away. I need to go home and rest."

"You need to be looked after." He glanced at me. "Fuck, you look pale as a skeleton, no, I mean spook...ghost. Pale as a ghost. What are they thinking making you go to work today?"

"They just wanted to debrief us."

"Then they should go to your house." He pulled a pair of shades from the dash and put them on. "So where are you living? At the airport hotel?"

"No, I'm in Eddington Gardens, not far from the rink."

"Yes, I know where that is. What number?"

"Eighty-six."

I closed my eyes. I felt like I was floating, dreaming. "Why did you come to the office?" I asked studying the way the sun intermittently flashed over my eyelids as we drove past a long row of palm trees.

"To get you."

"But...?"

"Shh." He rested his hand on my shoulder. "Talk later. Questions later. For now you need to rest."

I did as he'd suggested. My back was sore, the muscles were spasming, and my head ached. It was a relief to be in a soft chair, with my head resting. The hard plastic seat in the meeting hadn't been doing my bruised body any good.

I must have dozed with the sunshine warming me, because when I opened my eyes again Vadmir was helping me out of the car.

"Are your keys in your purse?" he asked.

"Yes."

"Can you walk?"

"Yes, I'm fine really." I swung my legs 'round and slid from his car to the floor. I thought my knees were going to support me but for some reason they just kept bending and folding.

"Hey, careful." He caught me and held me close. "You need help to walk."

"No, really...well okay, but it's just the painkillers I took. I'm not that injured, just a sore back and a sore head, a bit, well, I don't know really, it's all so..."

"Shh, you're okay now." He shut the door, and, still holding me upright, helped me into my apartment block.

* * * *

When I woke the sun was setting. I was in my own bed wearing just my underwear and facing the window. For a moment I lay there looking at the wash of colors streaking across the sky. There was a white airplane trail, a thick fluffy line fading into the distance.

I heard movement to my right and turned.

"Ah, shit," I muttered when my back complained.

"You are awake." Vadmir was sat in a big pink chair that I used for reading. He was holding his cell.

"Mmm, yes. How long have I been asleep?"

He glanced at his phone. "About eight hours."

"Really?"

"Yes, it is good for you to sleep. How are you feeling now?"

"Still a little sore." I licked my lips. "And thirsty."

He stood, walked up to me and smoothed his hand over my hair. "What would you like? Water? Coffee?"

"Coffee please."

He leaned down and touched his lips to my head, the way he used to when we were in Sokol. When he was mine and I was his.

I watched him leave the room then adjusted my pillows into a more comfortable, upright position. I realized that although my back was still sore, the spasm appeared to have gone from the muscles. Also everything didn't look so blurry, perhaps I'd gone a bit mad with the painkillers before the meeting, taken one too many.

I heard voices. Harmony was home. That was good. She needed rest, too.

Within minutes Vadmir was back holding two mugs of coffee. He handed one to me and then sat on the edge of the bed and took a sip of his.

I studied his face. A face I'd come to know so well but now didn't feel as if I knew at all. I thought back to watching him play. I'd felt so removed from him when he'd been down there, on the ice. I'd struggled to imagine it was the same man who'd sneaked into my bedroom and made love to me tenderly, quietly, and then made promises of more to come.

But my mind felt less fudged now, the painkillers having worn off, and I thought of how he'd barged into my work and stolen me away. Manhandled one of the company's top bosses and then threatened a security guy.

"Why the hell are you here?" I asked as a swarm of irritation prickled over me.

He frowned as though confused by my sudden outburst. "To see you."

"And so just like that you turn up." I rolled my eyes. "And grab me."

"Yes."

So he wasn't going to deny just turning up and accosting me then. "Well, how about last week? Didn't you want to see me then?"

He pressed his lips together and glanced out of the window.

"Last week," I said. "I wanted to see you. Hell, I was stupid enough to hang around waiting for you to call. You'd said you would. Crazy old me actually believed you."

"I'm sorry."

"Not good enough." I sipped my drink and let the reassuring, familiar flavor warm my mouth and throat. Inside, though, I still felt chilled by his week of silence. "Nowhere near good enough."

He frowned and shook his head.

"I haven't got the patience to be messed around by a guy who acts like he cares one minute but then can't follow up on a simple arrangement the next." I was on a roll now. "How hard could it be to pick up the phone? Even if you'd decided you didn't want to see me anymore, if something, or rather *someone* else had taken your fancy, it wouldn't have hurt to let me know." I wafted my hand in the air. "Oh, I know what we had was a whirlwind and not exactly conventional but still, you could have had the decency to end it rather than just let it fade into the horizon." I pointed out of the window with one hand and held the duvet over my bra with the other. My coffee sloshed dangerously near the edge of my cup.

"Sammy, I—"

"It's her, isn't it?" I braced for his reply. "Alena. You're back with her. I knew this would happen. How could you not swap her for me? She's Russian, your family love her. It just would have been nice to be told and—"

He'd pressed his hand over my mouth, the same way he had when we'd made love that last night in Sokol and I'd gotten too vocal.

"Be quiet," he said. "And listen."

I swallowed and glared at him.

He didn't remove his hand.

"I'm sorry I didn't call," he said, "It got complicated after you left. You are right. Alena did come back."

"Mmphf..." I managed behind his hand as I continued to glare at him.

"But it is not what you think."

I shoved at his arm and he dropped it away. "So tell me."

He rubbed his palm down the side of his face.

"So tell me what it is like," I said. "Because I have no damn idea why you're here if you're back with your ex."

"I'm not back with her." He went to reach for my hand but I pulled it away.

He sighed. "She'd been to see Darya, as you know, and then decided, after Darya had talked about America and her dreams of coming here, that she would like to move to Orlando with me." He paused and huffed. "She came to see me, said that she would move out here within the month and we could get married as we'd once planned. Have the family we'd talked about when we were growing up and that she'd never stopped loving me."

My belly quivered. I wasn't sure how long the coffee would stay down. Damn it. All my fears were being realized.

"But it's not like that for me," he said, "I tried to tell her no, I *did* tell her no, but it fell on deafness. She wouldn't believe that I wasn't in love with her anymore. She is so hooked on the idea that it will always be me and her and I couldn't convince her otherwise."

"So what happened?" I asked quietly and dreading the answer.

"She asked me to think about it. For one week." He put his mug on the locker and then did the same with mine. "I said that I would, but only to get her off my back."

"So you're considering it? Her coming out here to be with you?"

"No." He leaned forward and cupped my cheeks in his palms. "No, not for a second."

"So why..." His hands felt so right on me yet still I couldn't forget the pain of him not calling.

"I just needed to make that phone call, yesterday. Tell her that it wasn't happening, ever. I wanted that conversation out of the way before I saw you." He closed his eyes and shook his head. "And it was stupid of me. I should have called you, pushed Alena from my mind the way she had me all those years ago. But we have so much history and I'm not a cheat. I would never cheat. I'm a one-woman man."

I reached up and placed my hand over his. I was beginning to weaken for him.

"I felt like I'd been unfaithful to you, to her, too." He frowned. "I was in a mess all week, Sammy, I could hardly concentrate on the game. But I made the call yesterday morning. I put an end to it with her forever. I'd planned on coming to see you as soon as I could, make it up to you and hope you still liked me."

I pressed my hand over his. "Vadmir." His face had twisted with anxiety. I hated seeing him like this. He was usually so big and full of confidence. It reminded me of the time I'd seen him sitting alone in the bar in Moscow, pinching the bridge of his nose and his thoughts a million miles away.

"And then this." He swallowed tightly, as though he had cotton wool in his throat. "I'd just come out of practice yesterday and the crash was all over the news in the players' lounge. I felt sick."

"I'm okay."

He shook his head. "I could have lost you. Really lost you without ever having told you how I felt. And that fire officer, he..."

"He what?"

"He...that should have been me. I want to be there to save you, protect you. It should have been me at your side."

"You can't feel guilty about not being there," I said. "It's a fire officer's job to be on standby in case of emergency and he's trained to deal with it."

Vadmir leaned forward. He came so close I could see the flecks of darker blue in his irises. He didn't speak.

"And I'm trained for that kind of thing, too," I went on. "I don't just hand out drinks and duty free. I know the protocols for handling emergency situations."

He shook his head. "Well, it's too damn dangerous, this job of yours. It's got to change."

I pulled back and raised my eyebrows. "What?"

"I don't want you doing it."

"You can't tell me what to do, Vadmir." I pulled his hands from my face. "I'm my own person."

He shut his eyes and let out a long, low breath, seeming to deflate as he did so.

"And I happen to love my job," I said.

"So you want to get back on a plane? You want to get back in the air? Right now?"

I looked out of the window. A new jet engine trail was being made where the last one had faded. He'd forced me to think about something I'd been putting off bringing to the surface of my mind. "No. I don't." Saying the words made it real. I didn't want to get back onboard, not yet anyway.

"Then you won't have to."

"What do you mean?"

He rubbed his palm over his short hair creating a scratching sound in the quiet room. He then stood and went to the window.

I settled back on the pillow a little more, adjusting it so my spine was comfortable, and waited for him to explain. Once nestled into the softness I made the most of admiring the view. He had the tight, dark denims on that hugged his ass so well and certainly distracted me from thoughts of returning to work. Instead I licked my lips and remembered how soft the skin on his butt was.

"The thing is, Sammy," he said, turning to me.

"Mmm?" I quickly looked up at his face. "What?"

"I'm in love with you."

"I...I...what?" I stared at him. "You can't be."

"Why the hell not?" He shoved his hands onto his hips and frowned.

"Well, we...I don't know, we've only just met."

He walked over to the bed and sat down again. "No we haven't. I agree it's not months or years, but fuck, I hated not speaking to you. All I wanted was to have you by my side. Tell you about my day, find out how yours had been and then go to bed with you in my arms."

"So if you'd wanted all of that you should have called and explained." I huffed. "It wasn't exactly a great week for me, you know."

"Yes." He nodded. "I should have called and I am sorry."

"I didn't even have your cell number."

"You will have, from now on. I'll always be there, I promise."

"Oh, a famous Vadmir promise."

He tightened his jaw. "I always make good a promise."

"Not to me, you haven't." I thought of all the dirty, delicious things he'd said he'd do to my naked tied up body.

Suddenly his face softened. "Ah, I see." He slipped his hand behind my head, cradled my skull and hovered his lips over mine. "You're talking about *that* kind of promise."

I stared at his lips and wanted them on me. "You're not in love with me," I whispered, not daring to let myself fall for him any more than I already had. Love had been cruel to me in the past. I was loath to get burned again.

"I am so in love with you," he said. "When I thought something might have happened to you, when that picture of the plane burning was broadcast, I thought my heart would stop beating." He brushed his lips over mine. "I know you're not in love with me, not now, but maybe you could be. Maybe you will one day think I'm not such a stupid Russian boy and allow your heart to beat for mine."

My eyes prickled with tears and my chest tightened. "Vadmir," I managed. "You stupid Russian boy, can't you tell?"

"What?" He stroked his other hand down my cheek. "Can't I tell what?"

"I'm already in love with you."

Chapter Twenty-Two

Three Months Later

I studied the wake the *Dvoryantvo* was leaving in the ocean—a foamy white snake that traced our path. Like a plane's engine cloud, the trail dissolved with time.

A motorboat suited me well, as I hadn't been in the air since the crash. It wasn't that I would never fly again, I just hadn't needed to. After taking three weeks' sick leave and coping with the official complaint about Baron—he'd been formally cautioned for grabbing me—I'd been assigned to office duties. And now Vadmir had insisted I take vacation leave so we could spend time together off the Florida Keys. He'd been offered use of a wealthy Viper fan's luxury boat and been more than happy to take the fellow Russian up on the offer to show me the sights.

"How is the drink I made you, *milaya moya?*" Vadmir called from where he was steering on the top deck.

"Delicious." I used the straw to stir the brown sugar resting on the bottom of the long glass and then stretched my legs out on the lounger. "You've got the hang of these." The sun was hot but the breeze from the sea made it a perfect temperature for sunbathing. I adjusted my tiny white DKNY bikini bottoms—the top had yet to be unpacked—and checked on the progress of my sun-worshipping. Already I was topping up my tan quite nicely.

"I will anchor here so we can have lunch," he called.

"Perfect." I sipped my drink.

The boat slowed and the heat of the sun intensified. The noise of the engine quieted and Vadmir came down onto the deck. He wore dark navy swim shorts and a matching t-shirt. His shoulders had gone a little pink the day before and I'd insisted he cover up today.

"Did you see the island?" he asked, pointing toward the front of the boat. "I don't think it's inhabited."

I twisted to look at where he was indicating. A small rocky piece of land rose from the water just in front of us. It had a narrow, crescent-shaped beach, a few cliffs and appeared covered entirely by foliage. It looked idyllic and peaceful but there were no signs of life.

"No, I don't think anyone lives there," I agreed.

He set about dropping the anchor and I watched the muscles in his arms bunch as he completed his task. The boat drifted for a few yards and then I felt it catch.

He straightened and wiped his forearm over his forehead. "That should hold." He moved to where I was laying and sat on the lounger next to mine. A lazy smile crept over his face as he removed his shades and set them down. "You are getting a tan."

"Am I? Good." I put my drink aside, rested my head back and shut my eyes.

"I'm a bit worried about these, though," he said.

I opened my eyes just in time to see him circle my right nipple with his fingertip. Instantly it tingled and then tightened.

"Are you?" I said.

"Mmm." He reached with his other hand for my sun lotion. "Needs more of this."

He tipped a small white blob onto his index finger and then carefully and slowly rubbed it into my right nipple.

The weight in my breast increased. A familiar ache for more—more stimulation, more of him— crept over my flesh.

He spread the cream very precisely, smoothing it onto my now peaked nipple as though it was the most important job in the world.

A quiver attacked my belly and I pulled in a breath. Could life get any more perfect than being adored by the man I loved on a luxury boat?

"I should make sure the other one is protected," he said quietly. "It is my responsibility to look after you."

For a moment his touch left me and then my other nipple was treated to the same cool, sensual stimulation. That breast also grew heavy and again I shut my eyes and enjoyed everything about the moment.

I felt his shadow move across me and his lips brush mine.

"I hope you're not too hungry for lunch," he said, cupping the underside of my left breast.

I rested my hand on his shoulder and looked up into his eyes. "I'm only hungry for you."

"Good."

"Whoa, what are you doing?" He'd swung me up into the air. Quickly I locked my arms around his neck. "Vadmir?"

"You see out there." He walked to the bow of the boat, over where he'd just set the anchor. "There is no one, is there?"

I scanned the empty horizon. Not a soul to be seen. "No, there's no one."

He turned. "And the island, there is no one."

"I don't think so." I paused. He had a particularly wicked grin stretching his mouth wide and it made me suspicious. "What are you thinking, Russian boy?"

"I'm thinking..." He moved back past my lounger, up to the middle deck and into the main room of the boat. "That I can tie you to the bed and have my way with you and no one, not one person on this planet will hear your screams for more. You can be as loud and as wild as you want and there is only me to hear you."

I swallowed as he strode past the low, white leather seating in the galley.

"Well, it is isolated," I said, my pussy already trembling at the thought of being tied up. He'd kept promising this moment, over and over and now it was here. Had he orchestrated it so we'd be absolutely out of hearing distance from any other living being? Probably, he did seem to get what he wanted all of the time.

"And in here, Mrs. Arefyev, is where the magic will happen." He pushed the bedroom door with his foot and stepped inside.

I giggled. "I'm not Mrs. Arefyev yet, you know."

"You will be in six weeks."

"Yes, that's true." Again I glanced at the rock on my left ring finger. A single large diamond from Tiffany & Co. It was the most beautiful piece of jewelry I'd ever seen and certainly ever owned.

"You should get used to the name." He stooped and set me on the bed. "Because soon it will be yours forever."

"I can live with that."

He pushed a lock of hair over my ear and then turned to one of the cupboards. "Lay down," he ordered, his voice taking on a masterful tone that did funny things to my insides.

I dragged my gaze from his butt and did as he'd asked.

The bed was cool after lying in the sun and my skin slid on the silky sheets. Everything about the boat screamed luxury and opulence and was designer. I loved it.

Vadmir stood by the locker with a small cardboard box in his hands. I tried to read the label but couldn't make it out.

"I ordered some toys before we left," he said, studying the box's contents. "And now is the time to play with them."

"What did you get?" I asked, curiosity clawing at me.

I tried to sit but he placed his hand in the center of my sternum and pressed me flat on the bed. "Oh, no, you'll find out soon enough." He plucked a piece of purple velvet material into the air and then placed the box down.

"Close your eyes," he said, stretching the long, thin piece of material wide. "I want this to be a surprise for you."

My heart was beating fast and my pussy dampening. He wanted to take away my sight. It was a fantasy I'd been toying with and now he was going to make it real. But what else did he have in there? What else was he planning?

Again I did as he'd asked and closed my eyes.

Very gently and carefully he slid the blindfold beneath my head and fastened it. It was a neat fit and there was only blackness when I tried to peek.

"Is that comfortable?" he asked, stroking his finger down my cheek and then my neck.

"Yes."

"Good, now for your arms." He gripped my left wrist and hoisted it above my head. I pulled in a breath and squirmed as he attached it with soft material to the headboard. Fuck, he really was doing what he'd been talking about, finally. I could hardly wait for it to begin.

Without saying a word, he secured my opposite arm so I was spread before him, sightless and trapped.

"Oh, Sammy," he said, toying with my nipples again. "You do look beautiful."

"Fuck me," I said, wishing my bikini bottoms had gone already.

He chuckled. "I will when I'm ready. Right now I have the most perfect body set before me and all I want to do is play. Play with you and my new toys."

"What...what have you got?" Toys in the plural? What did he have in there?

"You'll soon find out."

Something about his tone made me nervous but I didn't have long to worry because he began to stroke and caress my body. Sliding his fingers over my breasts, my armpits, up my arms to my hands and back down again. I gasped as he resumed tweaking both of my nipples, pulling them to hard points.

Suddenly a hard, clasping sensation bit down on my right nipple.

"Ouch, I...what?"

"Shh," he spoke against my cheek, his stubble catching on my skin. "Just feel, go with it."

"But I…" It hurt, whatever he was doing, and it wasn't letting up. It felt like a clamp was attached to my nipple, squeezing and compressing. I tried to move my arms and examine it but I couldn't move them more than an inch.

"That's pretty," he said.

"What? What's pretty?"

"Nipple clamps. You'll like them, they have red stones in them and are pale gold."

My left nipple suddenly went on fire as the same harsh density jammed tight over it. Although the clamp hurt it was good hurt, it was the true stimulation I'd been craving when he'd been toying with me. I let the feeling collect and then fizz down my stomach and settle in my pelvis. My clit began to throb and my pussy tightened. This was working. I could do this.

"That is it, just right," he said, cupping my breasts and gently massaging them.

The weight of the clamps tugged at my flesh and I gasped. "Vadmir."

"I will make you feel fabulous all over," he said. "We have nowhere to be so do not be surprised if I take all day doing this."

"Yes, oh, but… damn, I want to fuck."

"I know you do." He pulled at my bikini bottoms, making fast work of removing them, and spread my legs wide. "I can smell how turned on you are, Sammy." I heard him breathe deep and sensed his weight at the base of the bed.

I twisted my head from left to right, wishing I could see him studying my pussy and sniffing my arousal.

"Shall we see how wet you are?" he asked. As he'd spoken he'd dragged his fingers through my folds and found my entrance. He pushed in, just a little. "Oh, yes, very wet."

I twitched my hips, wanting more and hoping he'd take the hint. He didn't, instead he removed his fingers.

I groaned in complaint.

Small kisses were planted on my right ankle, they journeyed upward, gliding over my knee and thigh.

Oh please God, let him give me an orgasm with his mouth.

His breaths were hot on my pussy and he was holding my thighs wide. I stilled completely, hoping for his tongue.

Suddenly it was there, sweeping up my pussy and then capturing my clit in a long, firm suction.

"Oh, Jesus yes," I said, arching my spine and pressing my head into the pillow. Again I tried to move my arms, only to be reminded that I couldn't.

He licked and sucked, laved and circled. He entered my pussy again with his fingers, filling me as he stoked my orgasm.

Bright lights flashed over my eyelids and my belly muscles tensed. I writhed and worked my body against the mattress. The nipple clamps dragged and created added stimulation to my already frenzied nerves.

"Yes, yes," I panted, "I'm coming..." Oh, it was just there, within reach.

He lifted up.

"Ah, ah, no, Vadmir, please..." I yanked my arms and tried to pull free. "What are you doing?"

My pussy was clenching around nothing, my clit throbbing for his mouth.

He rested his hand over my mound and pressed gently. "Shh, I'm just getting you ready for the big one."

"That was the big one, fuck, I was just about to—"

He silenced me with a kiss, a kiss that tasted of me.

"We have more toys to play with," he said. He leaned across me and I felt the bed give and then heard a rattle in the box. "How are you feeling, Sammy?"

"Frustrated," I huffed.

"Mmm, you should change that to relaxed."

"Relaxed? I was about to explode, how can I relax?"

"Oh, you will." Again he kissed me, everywhere, seemingly leaving no square inch unloved by his lips and tongue.

I lay there, sacrificial and with my breaths hard to catch. I tried to slow my wildly beating heart. The acute throb in my clit was unrelenting. I needed to come. He'd brought me so close.

His attention traveled lower over my stomach and then he pressed one teasing kiss over my clit.

I moaned and bunched the side of my face into my upstretched arm.

"Wider," he said, pushing my legs so far apart my hips ached. "And like this." He scooped my ass up and when he rested me back down there was the softness of a pillow beneath my buttocks. My hips were tilted now and I was bared open to him.

There was nowhere to hide.

Chapter Twenty-Three

"Vadmir, what are you doing?" I managed. The position was so sexy, sexy in a completely giving and trusting way. A mutual respect. I loved that I trusted him so much and I could be like this with him. I would never have dreamed of letting any other man see my body this vulnerable, see *me* this vulnerable, or give up control this way.

But Vadmir, he was different. Vadmir was the man I'd promised to marry. Vadmir respected me as I respected him.

"Now relax," he whispered, "just feel."

The shock of cool lube against my anus made me jerk.

"That's not relaxing," he said sternly. "Come on, Sammy, give it up. Let me have control of your body and of your pleasure."

"I'm trying."

"Try harder. You can do this."

I blew out a long low breath and forced my abdominal muscles to unwind. My focus, as I came to the end of the breath, settled on what Vadmir was doing. He was gently circling my asshole, rubbing and smoothing over the tight pucker. He enjoyed anal sex, a lot, and so did I. It was something we indulged in regularly. But we hadn't done it like this before, in broad daylight and with him watching his penetration of my hole.

"That's it, you're doing great," he soothed.

I bit down on my bottom lip.

There was a pressure at the center of my anus and then a steady smooth insertion. It wasn't his finger, though, it was flat-surfaced and growing ever wider.

"What?" I said, wriggling as the stretch heated up.

"Shh, it's a plug, let it fill you."

A plug! Damn, he really had gotten imaginative when shopping. "God, it feels so..."

"What? Tell me."

"Cool and big and...getting bigger."

"Nearly there."

"You know I'm going to return the favor with this...right?"

He chuckled. "I can't wait."

I pursed my lips and blew out a breath. I couldn't take much more, the denseness inside my rectum and the flare of the plug was all getting too much. "Vadmir, I can't..."

"Shh, almost...there..."

"Ah, ah..."

It popped in and my asshole clamped around the base. I shifted on the bed and the sensation just moved with me.

"Good girl," he said, kissing my patch of pubic hair. "Good, good girl." His kiss moved downward and again he suckled on my clit.

I moaned and my legs flopped wider still. Instantly the need to orgasm was hurtling toward me again. I'd been hovering and now I was speeding toward it.

He lifted his head. "I want your mouth," he said. "Take me."

I wailed in annoyance that my climax hadn't arrived but the sound was barely out and his cock was prodding at my lips.

Quickly I opened up. Greedy as always for his taste.

He slid in, the thickness of him filling my mouth as he supported the base of my neck, holding me to him.

"Ah yes, *dah, dah*," he moaned.

I wished I could see him. I adored the dreamy expression he always got when I sucked him off. But for today I was blind—blind and buzzing with need.

"I love fucking your mouth," he said, sinking deep but not so much that I gagged. He knew his full length would do that to me. "And I love fucking your ass, but your pussy, that's my favorite part of you to fuck, Mrs. Arefyev. Your hot, tight pussy. You want me to do that now, don't you? While your ass is full you want my dick in your cunt."

I nodded the best I could. It was absolutely what I wanted and I couldn't wait to experience the sensation of being stuffed full in both holes.

But wait I did. Vadmir was in no hurry to fuck my cunt and he continued to ride in and out of my mouth. He spoke in Russian several times, low, grunting words that I couldn't decipher even though I knew more of his language each day.

Finally, he withdrew and settled above me. I searched for his mouth and he captured mine with his. As our tongues tangled I wondered if he enjoyed the flavor of himself that I passed to him.

"I'm going to make you come so hard," he said, breaking the kiss and easing his cock into me. "So hard you will be heard screaming in America."

"Yes, yes..." God it was a tight fit. He'd only just started to penetrate me and the hot flesh of his cock was stretching my pussy. My full ass had diminished the available space in my pussy.

"I love no condoms," he muttered. "I love you all hot and wet on my skin."

"Yes," I managed. "Hot and wet."

He prodded higher but didn't get far. "Rest your muscles, let me inside you."

"I'm trying, I'm so... so turned on. I want to come."

"And you will soon, let me fill you up first." Again he curled his hips under. This time he had more success and eased into my wet channel.

I groaned. It was a loud chesty sound that I let erupt from my throat.

He matched it with a groan of his own and sank to full depth.

"Vadmir, oh God, yes!" I shouted, yanking my arms and locking my legs around the backs of his thighs. "Fuck, that's so much."

And it was. I was so full of him. The divine fullness in my ass and his thick cock in my pussy had made me forget where I ended and he began. "Fuck me. Fuck me. Fuck me."

I didn't need to shout instructions because he was already doing just that. He was pumping in and out of me. Each shunt dragging his pubis over my clit and thrusting me up the bed.

Sweat popped on my body and my shoulders hurt from the strain of fighting my bondage. I got lost in the Technicolor flashing behind the blindfold.

My orgasm was there and I screamed with the relief of finally coming.

Still Vadmir kept on fucking me. His energy increased as if spurred on by my climax.

My breasts, still heavy with the clamps, jiggled and swayed and my pussy spasmed and clenched his cock. My breaths were hard to catch and my pulse was thumping to a crazy tempo in my ears.

"Again," he said, biting at my neck and then my collarbone. "Again."

He bashed against my clit and before I knew it his thudding, thrusting rhythm had me orgasming again. I wailed his name and clenched my fists. On and on it went like waves washing over me, each one a swarm of pleasure. I bucked and squirmed wanting more and taking it.

"Ah, that's it, that's it, now me..." he said. With one forceful surge he buried deep and released his cum.

I was hot and trembling and my mind a haze of ecstasy. I tightened my hold on him with my legs and rejoiced in his semen discharging into my body.

He gave three more powerful lunges, gasping my name each time, and then stopped.

For a few minutes we said nothing. We were just frozen in our joined position catching our breaths and enjoying the final pulses of pleasure that trembled over our flesh.

"That was amazing," he said, finally pulling out. "And good that no one could hear you."

I giggled. "What I that loud?"

"Yes." He set a hot kiss over my lips and then tugged off the blindfold.

I blinked in the sudden bright light. I'd been lost in my own dark world that consisted only of sensations.

"Do you like these?" he asked, cupping my breast just beneath the clamps.

I looked down. "Oh, very pretty." As he'd said they were gold with rubies set in them. "Are they staying on?"

"No, they'll get too hot in the sun, but another time you can wear them for the whole day."

I shifted my arms. "Can you undo me?"

"No."

"Why not?" I looked up at his face. His cheeks were red and his lashes had lightened a little in the sunshine but his eyes were still flashing with wicked ideas.

"Because I haven't finished with you yet."

He hadn't? Oh Jesus, I wasn't sure how much I could take. I'd just had the most wonderful multiple orgasm at the hands of an expert tormentor.

"What else is there?" I asked, suddenly feeling a little nervous.

"When these come off it's going to be intense," he said, touching the right nipple clamp. "I want you to enjoy that."

He slid his other hand between my legs and gently rubbed over my super-sensitive clit.

I moaned and thought about shifting away but then stayed. I liked his touch too much.

"Come again," he said.

"I can't."

"You can, I want you to." He kissed over the clamp. "And I'm not untying you until you do."

"Oh God."

"He won't save you."

My clit was vibrating under his touch, the first spark of pressure building.

"Like this," he said, suddenly releasing the right clamp.

"Oh fuck," I shouted. A mass of swirling, boiling heat shot from my nipple to my clit. It was as if all the blood stored there was pure potent pleasure.

"Come," he said, upping the speed of his fingers.

I did. It was there. It grabbed me and thrust my body up and then down the bed. The butt plug shifted, increasing the tension in my pelvis and giving my innards something solid to spasm against.

He released the other clamp and the sensation doubled.

I screamed again, wailed and called his name.

His mouth hit down on mine in a passionate kiss. He captured my cries of pleasure and continued to eke them from me.

My clit was bubbling with release. I'd never felt anything like it. My body was singing to his tune, doing exactly what he wanted it to do, it was out of my control. He was in me, on me and shooting ecstasy through me.

"Ah, ah, Vadmir," I said, a sob bubbling up from my chest. "It's so much. Too much. No more."

He lifted up and with one quick tug my arms were free and my clit no longer being stimulated.

A single tear rolled down my cheek.

"Hey, hey, I'm sorry, I didn't mean to—" He dragged me close and curled his arms and legs around me.

"Shh..." I pressed my index finger to his lips. "Don't say sorry."

"But you have a tear." He caught it on his thumb. "Why are you crying? Did it hurt in a bad way?"

"No. No it was all good. I'm just..."

"What?" His brow creased. "What is it? Tell me."

"I'm just so happy that I can be like this with you."

"Like what?" A small smile crept onto his lips.

"That we can trust each other so much."

"I love that, too. And damn, you are the sexiest, most responsive, giving woman on the planet and I can't wait to make you my wife."

"It won't be long."

"No, and in the meantime..."

"What?"

"We need to carry on rehearsing the wedding night," he said.

"I like the sound of that."

He slid his hand down my back and rested it over the crack of my ass cheeks. "Which might include, as you suggested, you tying me to the bed and doing whatever you want."

I grinned and clenched around the plug. My pelvis shuddered and another tremor of bliss shivered its way over my body. The idea thrilled me as much as what we'd just done.

"I think this is definitely something we'll take turns at." I stroked my finger down his cheek and rested it over his sternum. "And I can't wait to have your sexy body to play with, I think you're going to like it."

He laughed. "I think you're going to be a tease."

"What like you were?"

"I hardly teased you at all." He looked indignant.

"Oh, you really did."

He suddenly rolled me over so that I was on top of him. "I love you," he said, capturing my cheeks in his hands.

"*Ya tebya lyublyu*," I whispered onto his lips.

He pushed my hair over my ears and grinned. "You learnt it in Russian."

"Of course. Our bodies speak the same language, it's about time our tongues did, too."

He smiled and kissed me again. It seemed our tongues spoke the same language already, and as I let myself get lost in him I marveled at how lucky I'd been to catch myself a hot Russian boy who was pretty damn nifty with a hockey stick and who also could keep up with me in the bedroom.

THE END

About Hot Ice

If you loved RUSSIAN HEAT grab the other books in the HOT ICE series.

HIRED

CROSS-CHECKED

SLAP SHOT

TEAMWORK

HIGH-STICKED

MISCONDUCT

RUSSIAN HEAT

About Lily Harlem

Based in the UK Lily Harlem is an award-winning, USA Today best-selling author of sexy romance. She's a complete floozy when it comes to genres and pairings writing from heterosexual kink, to gay paranormal and everything in-between. She's also very partial to a happily ever after.

One thing you can be sure of, whatever book you pick up by Ms Harlem, is it will be wildly romantic and deliciously sexy. Enjoy!

.

Made in the USA
Middletown, DE
22 November 2020